THE GUNSMITH

432

The Bank Job

THE GUNSMITH

432

The Bank Job

J.R. Roberts

SPEAKING VOLUMES, LLC
NAPLES, FLORIDA
2018

The Bank Job

ISBN 978-1-62815-752-9

Chapter One

The Bank of Truxton, Nebraska had three tellers: two women and one man. The women were older, in their 40's, but the man was young, in his 30's. He smiled, engaged the customers while he served them, and seemed well liked by his workmates.

Clint had seen the man before, ten years earlier, with three other men. When he robbed a bank in Ten Pines, Missouri.

And now here, in Nebraska, the man was working in the bank. Perhaps, as he got older, he'd developed a talent for planning robberies, rather than just running hurried, unplanned, unrehearsed jobs. That made more sense than thinking the man had gone straight, and was now a simple bank teller.

But Clint had a bank draft he needed to cash, and wasn't going to let the presence of the former bank robber keep him from cashing it. After all, he wasn't making a deposit, so he didn't have to worry about this man stealing his money along with everyone else's.

He thought about going to one of the women, but decided instead to go to the man. Maybe he was wrong, and on closer inspection, it would be a different face.

Maybe . . .

***

The teller saw Clint walk into the bank, and frowned. He looked familiar, but where from? Someplace in his past, of course, someplace he didn't want brought up just now. Maybe the man would go to Tilly, or Beth's . . . but no. He was walking straight for Mark Crawford's window.

He smiled . . .

"Good-afternoon, sir," the teller said. "Can I help you?"

"Yes, I need to cash this." Clint handed the man the draft.

"Certainly, sir. Do you bank with us?"

"No, I don't," Clint said, "but it's drawn on an account here."

The teller looked at it and said, "Ah, I see, sir. Mr. Jameson's account. He's one of our best customers."

"Yes, he is."

Dave Jameson was the biggest rancher in the county, and Clint had done him a big favor—a favor Jameson insisted on paying for.

"So there won't be a problem?" Clint asked.

"No, sir, not at all," the teller said.

"Good. How long have you been working here?"

The younger man looked directly into Clint's eyes.

"Excuse me?"

"I'm just making conversation," Clint said.

"Oh, well, I've been here only a few weeks. Before that I worked in other banks, in other places."

"I see," Clint said. "Have you always been interested in banks?"

The teller smiled. "I'll be right back, sir. This amount will have to come out of the safe, and I need the manager for that."

2

"I'll be patient," Clint promised.

The teller smiled again, turned and went to the bank manager's office.

Clint was convinced, now that he had a closer look, that this was the same man who had robbed the bank in Missouri. Now the question was, had he gone straight, or was he setting this bank up to be robbed?

***

The teller returned with an older gentleman in tow.

"Mr. Adams?" the man asked.

"That's right."

"I'm Nathan Winslow, the bank manager. Would you come into my office, please?"

"Is there a problem?"

"I'd just prefer to handle a transaction of this amount in private," Winslow said. "That is, if you agree."

"Sure," Clint said, "why not?"

Winslow led the way, then allowed Clint to proceed him into the office.

"Close the door, Mark. Thank you."

Clint sat so that the teller was not behind him. The young man was standing just in front of the door with his hands clasped.

"I hope you understand that transactions this large aren't usually conducted right out front," Winslow said. "For obvious reasons."

3

"Such as?" Clint asked. He wondered what precautions a bank would take when it had already hired a bank robber to be a teller?

"Well . . . we don't need it to be known that this much money changes hands out in the open."

"I see." Should I inform Mr. Winslow of the teller's past, or give "Mark" the benefit of the doubt that he might have gone straight in the ensuing years.

"So, if you'll wait here," the manager said, "I'll just get your money from the safe and pay you in my office."

"That's fine," Clint said.

"Mark, will you look after Mr. Adams while I fetch his money?"

"Of course, sir."

Winslow left the office.

"Does he know?" Clint asked.

"Know what, sir?"

"About your past."

"My past? You mean, my work history? Oh, yes, sir—"

"No," Clint said, "I mean about your bank robbery history."

"My bank—I don't understand, Mr. Adams. What are you saying?"

"I'm saying I saw you hold up a bank in a small Missouri town ten years ago. What were you, twenty then? Have you gone straight?"

"Sir," the teller said, "I think you have me mixed up with someone else. I hope you don't intend to tell Mr. Winslow that I'm a . . . a bank robber!"

Clint studied the young man for a few moments, then decided to let it go, for now.

"You know, you're probably right," he said. "I think I may have you mixed up with somebody else."

The younger man heaved a sigh of relief.

"Thank you, sir," he said. "You sure had me scared there, for a minute."

"Sorry, kid," Clint said.

Winslow reentered the office, carrying a brown envelope, thick with money. He sat behind his desk with it.

"Are you sure, Mr. Adams, you wouldn't like to open an account with us? This money would certainly be safer in the bank."

"I don't think so, Mr. Winslow," Clint said. "I think I'll just take my money and be on my way. I actually am having supper tonight with Mr. Jameson."

Well," Winslow said, "I hope you'll tell Mr. Jameson how cooperative we've been."

"Oh, you can be sure," Clint said, accepting the envelope. "Mr. Jameson will hear all about this at supper."

Chapter Two

Clint left the bank, wondering what his next move should be.

He had tracked down three men who had stolen a hundred head of cattle and brought them and the herd back, alone. Along the way he'd taken a few bumps and bruises while doing it. Once he finished his job for Dave Jameson the rancher insisted that he be his guest for a few days of R&R. But now it was time for him to get back to the real world.

He took a room in the Truxton House Palace, put his horse up in the livery, and then went to the bank to cash in his payment.

He told Jameson, who was an old friend, that payment wasn't necessary, but the man insisted not only on payment, but on a big payment. So Clint was now walking around with two thousand dollars on him. If he had even given a thought to opening an account in the bank, seeing the teller, Mark Crawford, convinced him not to. He didn't know if that was really the young man's name, but he was certain of the face. It was the man he'd seen hold up the bank ten years before in Ten Pines, Missouri.

Should he go to the sheriff of Truxton? Since he'd brought the rustlers to justice when the lawman couldn't, there was no love lost there. Sheriff Jack Irving didn't want Clint in town, which was, of course, one of the reasons he was there. He wasn't about to let a second-class lawman post him outside the town limits.

So no, he wouldn't be going to Sheriff Irving about the bank robber working at the bank. Maybe he'd send some telegrams—specifically to his friends Rick Hartman in Labyrinth, Texas, and Talbot Roper in Denver—to see what, if anything, they knew about a man named Mark Crawford.

Also, since he was having supper with Jameson at the town's Cattleman's Club he'd see what, if anything, the rancher knew about the bank, the bank teller and the manager.

But until then he decided to take up a position in the saloon right across the street from the bank, where he could keep an eye on the front door. If Crawford came out, he'd follow him. And if any suspicious riders approached the bank, he'd be ready for anything.

If nothing happened, at least he'd have a few beers and kill some time before his supper.

***

After Clint Adams left with his money, "Mark Crawford" remained in the bank manager's office, taking a seat.

"He knows," he said to Winslow.

"Knows what?"

"He recognized me."

"From where?" the older man asked.

"I was part of a gang that held up a bank in Ten Pines, Missouri ten years ago."

"And he was there?"

"Apparently."

"Did you confirm it for him?"

"No," Crawford said, "I denied it, told him he had me mixed up with somebody else."

"And what did he say?"

"He apologized."

"So he believed you?"

"Maybe," Crawford said, "but I think we're gonna have to wait and see."

"Well," Winslow said, "why don't you go back out to your cage and finish your day's work. I'll talk to the sheriff about the Gunsmith."

Crawford nodded and stood up.

"I don't need him on my back, you know," he said.

"I understand," Winslow said. "We'll do what we can."

Crawford nodded again, and then left the office.

Chapter Three

By closing time at the bank, the teller still hadn't put in an appearance. The fact that he didn't immediately run might have meant something. Or else he was simply smart enough not to run, and expose himself.

Clint finished his third beer and left the saloon under curious eyes. He hadn't spoken to anyone but the bartender for the two hours he'd been in there. Most of the patrons of the Black Horse Saloon found that odd.

"Who was that guy?" one of them asked the bartender.

"I don't know," the barman said, "but he was really interested in the front door of the bank."

The man looked out across the street.

"It's closed now."

"Yeah," the bartender said, "and he left. You know, Jake, I think maybe you ought to go get the sheriff."

"Yeah, Leo," Jake said, "I think maybe you're right."

"And don't tell him anythin' until he gets here," Leo said. "I wanna tell him myself."

"Sure, Leo," Jake said, "sure."

Jake ran from the saloon and headed for the sheriff's office.

***

When Jake ran into the office, Sheriff Irving looked up from his desk.

"What's the rush?" he asked. He was a bearded man in his 40s who did as little work as possible in his job—until an election year.

"Leo, over at the Black Horse wants to see ya, Sheriff."

"What about?"

"He didn't want me to say," Jake answered, "but it's got somethin' to do with the bank."

"The bank, huh?"

"Yeah," Jake said, then couldn't hold it in. "Some guy was using the saloon to case it."

"All right," Irving said. He stood, took his gunbelt from a peg on the wall, and then his hat. "Let's go."

***

"Who was he?" Irving asked Leo.

"You told him?" Leo asked Jake.

"He made me."

"Go sit and finish your beer," Irving told Jake.

"Sure, Sheriff."

Leo gave him a fresh one, and he took it to a table. The place was starting to fill up, and the covers had come off the gaming tables.

"Whataya got for me?" Irving asked.

"There was a man here, standing at the bar, nursing beers and watchin' the bank."

"And you think he was casin' it?"

"Well, when the bank closed, he left."

"What'd he look like?"

"Tall fella, not young but not old, wore a gun like he knew how to use it—"

"Ah, Jesus!"

"What?"

"That's the Gunsmith."

"He's in town?"

Irving nodded.

"He's doin' business with Jameson."

"Why would he be watchin' the bank?"

"I don't know," Irving said, "but I guess I'll have to find out."

"I never heard nothin' about the Gunsmith robbin' banks," Leo said.

"Me, neither," Irving said, "but there's always a first time."

Chapter Four

"You saw what?" Dave Jameson asked.

"A bank robber working in your bank," Clint said. "I went in to cash the draft you gave me, and he was there, working as a teller."

"Jesus!" Jameson swore. "Did you tell Winslow, the manager?"

"No," Clint said, "but I talked to the teller."

"What'd he have to say?"

"That I made a mistake."

"And what did you say?"

"I agreed," Clint said.

"So you changed your mind?"

"No," Clint said, "I just want him to think I changed my mind. He's the man I saw ten years ago—older, but it's him."

"So what are you gonna do? Talk to the sheriff?"

"He's useless," Clint said. "You told me that when you asked for my help."

"That's true. Maybe I should talk to Winslow, then."

"I'm going to watch this fella a little closer for a while," Clint said, "since I'm in no hurry to move on."

Clint cut into his steak, found that it bled perfectly, and tasted just as good.

"And this steak might keep me here longer, too," he admitted.

"I'm glad you like it," Jameson said, "but I'm more concerned with what you found at the bank. I wish you'd become more active in findin' out just what the hell is happenin'. Why is he workin' there?"

"Well," Clint said, "if you want to talk to the manager about it, I'll talk to the teller, Crawford."

"Was that his name back then?"

"I don't know," Clint said. "It's not like he was with the James Gang, or Younger Gang. They were just a bunch of kids who decided to rob a bank."

"Were they caught?"

"I really don't know," Clint said. "I didn't join the posse that chased them, and I didn't stay in town long enough to learn what happened. All I know is that I saw this man, whatever his name is."

"And you're sure?"

"Dead sure."

"All right, then," Jameson said, "how about a shot of whiskey with this steak, and then a cold mug of beer?"

"Sounds great," Clint said.

***

Mark Crawford went to his room at the rooming house, changed out of his work clothes, and then took a walk to the River Run Saloon. While the Black Horse had girls and gambling, the River Run had only girls. And Crawford was interested in one in particular.

He entered the saloon, which was about three quarters full with the crowd still growing. The gamblers went to the Black Horse, but the drinkers came to River Run. He took a table and waited. Eventually, she came over.

"Bad day?" she asked.

"The worst," he said. "Bring me a whiskey and sit with me."

"You'll have to buy me drinks."

"I'll pay the price."

She nodded, went to the bar and told the bartender, "A shot of whiskey and a glass of champagne."

He put them on her tray and said, "Attagirl, Stacy."

She took the drinks back to Crawford's table and sat across from him.

He didn't down the whiskey in one gulp, but rather sipped it as she did her champagne. The drinks were just a prop, a way for them to talk to each other without people realizing how well they knew each other. They had come to town separately and gotten their jobs, while pretending only to see each other in the saloon. So all anyone ever saw was the pretty brunette talking to another drunk.

"What's goin' on?" she asked.

"The Gunsmith came into the bank today."

"So?"

"So . . . he recognized me."

"As what, and from where?"

"He recognized me from a bank job I pulled in Ten Pines, Missouri ten years ago."

"Ten years?" she asked. "You were a baby."

14

"I was nineteen and it was my first job," he said.

"Did he tell your boss?"

"I don't think so," Crawford said. "I mean, Mr. Winslow didn't say anything."

"But you did?"

"I hadda tell him!" he snapped.

"Calm down, Lance," she said, using his real name. "Did the Gunsmith say anythin' to you?"

"Yes, he told me he recognized me," he said. "I denied it and told him he had the wrong man."

"Did he buy it?"

"He said he did, but I don't know."

"Look," she said, reaching out to touch his hand, but then pulling back before anyone could see. "We have a plan and we have to stick to it."

"I know that."

"If he approaches you again, just play it the same way. He's made a mistake, you don't know what he's talkin' about. Got it?"

"Got it."

"Keep me informed on what's happenin'," she said, standing up.

"Yeah, okay."

"And stay calm," she said. "You want a beer?"

"Sure."

"Just sit tight."

She went to get a beer, watched while the bartender drew it. He was obviously agitated. She wondered if she was going to have to sleep with him tonight in order to calm him down and make him feel like a big man?

"There ya go," the bartender said, setting the beer on her tray.

"Thanks."

She carried it back to the table, hoping it would do the trick and keep sex from becoming necessary.

Chapter Five

When Clint and Jameson had devoured their steaks, the waiter took the plates away and brought them pie and coffee. It wasn't peach, but wild berry would do the trick.

"I have a question," Jameson said.

"What is it?"

"Why don't you just tell the sheriff and then take your money and leave?" the rancher asked. "It's not your responsibility to keep the bank safe, it's his."

"That's true," Clint said, "but I can't help feeling I've walked into the middle of something."

"And you just can't walk away, huh?"

Clint shook his head.

"Leave it to you to get involved where you don't have to," he said.

"I know," Clint said. "It's a flaw."

Jameson picked up his coffee and saluted Clint with the mug.

"Let's just hope it's not a fatal flaw," he said.

Clint picked up his own mug and said, "I'll drink to that."

While they were enjoying their coffee, a man came over to Jameson and whispered in his ear.

"What's going on?" Clint asked.

"There's somebody here to see us," Jameson said.

"Who?"

"The sheriff."

"What's he want?"

"We'll have to let him in to ask," the rancher said. "Unless you want him to wait outside?"

"No," Clint said, "I guess we can let him in."

"Bring him in, Silas," Jameson said to the man.

"Yes, sir."

The man left the dining room and returned moments later with Sheriff Irving.

"I appreciate you seein' me, Mr. Jameson," Irving said.

"Pull up a chair, Sheriff, and tell us what's on your mind," Jameson invited.

"I'm actually here to talk to Mr. Adams," the sheriff said.

"Well, there he is," Jameson said, pointing. "Talk to 'im. By the way, do you want some coffee?"

"No, thanks," Irving said. "I'm fine."

"What's on your mind, Sheriff?" Clint asked. "I thought we did all the talking we were going to do when I came to town and asked you about the rustlers."

"Well, this is about somethin' else," the lawman said. "Seems some folks in town have noticed that you have a special interest in our bank."

"Which one?" Clint asked. "There're two banks in town, aren't there?"

"I'm talkin' about the big one," Irving said, "where Mr. Jameson, here, banks."

"Ah, well," Clint said, "Mr. Jameson rewarded me for bring back his cattle, and I went into the bank to cash it."

"I see. Then you came out, went to the Black Horse Saloon and watched the front doors of the bank until it closed."

Clint stared at the man.

"Are you asking me if I was casing the bank?" he asked. "Planning a robbery?"

"I'm just doin' my job," Irving said. "Checking up on somebody who was showin' special interest in the bank."

Clint looked at Jameson, who simply shrugged.

He wasn't sure how to handle the situation, but decided to keep the sheriff in the dark a little bit longer, until he could talk to the teller again.

"I was just killing some time, having a few beers, and staring out the window, Sheriff," he said. "Is there a law against that?"

"No, sir, there ain't," Irving said. "If you're tellin' me that's all it was, then I'll believe you."

"That was it," Clint said.

There was a moment, which turned into a few moments, when the three of them sat there silently.

"Is there anythin' else, Sheriff," Jameson finally asked.

"No, sir," Irving said, "That was it." He stood up. "Ya'll can go back to your pie and coffee now. Thanks for the time."

The sheriff left the dining room.

"Now what do you suppose caused that man to suddenly, decide to do his job?" Clint asked.

"Beats me," Jameson said. "I wonder who saw you watching the bank?"

"Could've been anybody in that saloon," Clint said, "or the bartender, playing the concerned citizen."

"Folks in this town tend to mind their own business," Jameson observed.

"Well," Clint said, "somebody sure wasn't."

"For a minute I thought you were gonna tell him about the bank robber teller."

"I want to talk to the kid first," Clint said. "I guess there's still the possibility that he's gone straight."

"You really think so?" Jameson asked. "And it's just a co-incidence that he works in a bank?"

"I don't know," Clint said, "but that's what I want to find out."

Chapter Six

Clint and Jameson left the Cattleman's Club, stopping on the steps outside. Around them the town was settling in for the evening, many people going home for the night, and others heading for saloons.

"That's where you're gonna find him," Jameson said, pointing across the street at a small saloon. "Not that one, exactly, but at a saloon. Where else would a bank teller go after work?"

"If he's not married."

"Yeah, that's another thing," Jameson said. "If he's married, he may very well have settled down and gone straight."

"See? I've got things to find out about him."

"Well, if I was you I'd go look in the River Run. There's no gambling there, and I don't think a bank teller goes from work to the Black Horse Saloon to gamble."

"Thanks for the advice," Clint said. "I'll go and check it out first."

"And you know where I am if you need anythin'," Jameson said.

The two men shook hands and went their separate ways.

***

Clint took Jameson's advice and went to the River Run Saloon first. For a place that didn't feature gambling it was pretty packed. Men lined the bar, and all the tables seemed to be taken. The thing about saloon bars, though, is that there was always room for one more.

Clint elbowed his way to a place at the bar and waved down the bartender.

"Beer," he said.

"You betcha," the man said. He went off and came back with a frosty mug for Clint, setting it down in front of him.

Clint picked up his mug, sipped, and then turned to examine the room. There were several girls working the floor, delivering drinks, laughing with the men and dancing away from their grabbing hands.

And then he saw him.

The young teller had obviously gone home, changed his clothes, and come to the saloon for drinks. He had two empty mugs in front of him, and was working on a third.

His own mug in hand, Clint walked over to the table.

"Hello, Mark," he said.

The man looked up at him, squinting even though it wasn't particularly bright or smoky in the room.

"Is that Clint Adams?" he asked.

"Yes, it is."

"You sit down here, Mr. Adams," Mark said, pulling out a chair. "Sit and have a beer with me."

"Don't mind if I do."

Clint sat directly across from the teller, with his left shoulder against the wall.

"What brings you here?" Mark asked.

"I was looking for you."

"For me?" Mark asked. "I'm flattered. How did you know I'd be here?"

"I didn't," Clint said. "I was just checking saloons and here you are."

"And why were you lookin' for me?" Mark asked. "Oh, wait. Don't tell me you still think I'm a bank robber?"

"I don't know," Clint said. "Are you? Or were you?"

"Look, Mr. Adams," Mark said, staring at Clint with glassy eyes, "I'm a bank teller, plain and simple."

"You're not married, are you Mark?" Clint asked.

"Married. Hell no!" Mark said. "Why would I get married? I don't need a wife. Why would you ask me that?"

"Just wondering."

"Well, you can stop wonderin' about that," Mark said. "No wife."

"And what about your career as a bank robber?" Clint asked. "Why did you decide to give that up?"

"You know that—" Mark started, but then he stopped and grinned. "You're sneaky."

"Am I?"

"I never said I was a robber."

"No," Clint said, "I said that."

"Hello, boys." One of the saloon girls came over and put an arm around Mark's shoulders. It looked to Clint like she was squeezing him pretty tightly.

"Adams," Mark said, "meet . . . Stacy."

"Adams?" she asked.

"Clint Adams."

She took her arm away from Mark's shoulders and pointed at Clint.

"The Gunsmith?"

"I'm afraid so."

"And you know Mark?"

"Actually, I don't," Clint said. "I just met him today, at the bank."

"And you're buyin' him a drink," she said. "How nice."

"Not exactly," Clint said. "We were just . . . talking."

"That's funny," Stacy said, then looked at Mark. "Didn't you tell me you were goin' home?"

"Huh? Oh, yeah, yeah," Mark said, "time for me to go home to bed. Gotta go to work tomorrow." He stood up. "Nice talkin' to ya, Adams."

He turned and left the saloon.

Stacy sat in his seat and smiled at Clint.

"Buy _me_ a drink?"

Chapter Seven

Clint agreed to buy Stacy a drink because, judging just from the short exchange she had with Mark Crawford, he felt she knew him. And if that was the case, maybe she wasn't what she was pretending to be, either.

He didn't see a woman with the bank robbers in Missouri ten years ago, but that didn't mean she wasn't one. The bank teller and the saloon girl. Were they going straight, or planning a robbery?

"Does the owner tell you to drink champagne with customers because it's expensive?" he asked, indicating the glass in front of her.

"What? Oh, no, I just like champagne," she said, picking the glass up. "I guess I have expensive tastes."

"Well," he said, "to develop those tastes you must have experienced them, before. Maybe when you had a lot of money?"

"Me? A lot of money? My family was so poor—but never mind. No, if I had money would I be working this job?" She put her glass down and spread her arms. "Why would anyone want to be a saloon girl if they had money?"

"So then why not do something else?" he asked.

"Like what?"

"Be a bank teller."

Stacy laughed.

"I have one talent, Mr. Adams," she said. "This is it. Look pretty in a dress." Then she gave him a sloe-eyed look. "Or maybe two things. Care to find out. Upstairs?"

"No, thanks," he said. "Don't get me wrong. You're very pretty, but I don't make it a habit of paying women to be with me."

"No," she said, "I guess you don't. Why would you ever have to. I'll bet some women have wanted to pay you."

"Are you offering?" he asked.

She laughed. "Sorry, but I haven't been able to get into the habit of givin' it away, so I guess we have a high wall between us."

"I guess we do," Clint said. "Another glass of champagne?"

"Please," she said, putting down her empty glass.

Clint had two more beers with Stacy, until one of the other girls, a cute blonde, came over and complained.

"This place is crazy, Stacy, and Lila and I are doin' all the work. Get off your ass!" She smiled at Clint. "Sorry."

"No problem," Clint said.

"I gotta go," Stacy said, standing up. "Thanks for the drink."

She started to go off to work, but Clint looked at the blonde and said, "Buy you a drink?"

"Well, sure, honey," she said, taking Stacy's chair.

"Would you bring my friend a drink?" Clint asked Stacy.

"Sure thing," she said. "That's my job." She looked at the blonde, who was several years younger than she was, and asked, "What would you like, Angela?"

"I think I'll have a glass of champagne, thank you."

"Comin' up," Stacy said. "How about you, Mr. Adams? Another beer?"

"I'll just finish this one," he said, holding up his half empty mug.

Stacy rushed off to the bar and came back with a glass of champagne on a tray. For a moment Clint feared she might dump it in Angela's lap, but in the end she simply plucked it off the tray and set it in front of the girl.

"Thank you, Stacy."

"Just let me know if you want anything else," Stacy said, and went off to work.

"Now you can take a little time off your feet—" Clint said.

"Yes, thank you."

"—and tell me everything you know about Stacy."

Chapter Eight

According to Angela, Stacy had come to town only months before and gotten her job at the River Run.

"Was Mark Crawford here, already?"

"Who?"

"The bank teller who comes in here."

"We got lots of men who come in here," she said. "I don't know all their names."

"I was just sitting here with him?"

"Oh, that fella?" she asked. "I thought he was a friend of yours."

"So he's not a good friend of Stacy's?"

"Not that I know of," Angela said. "To tell you the truth, she ain't got no men friends. And she don't take any men up to her room."

"Really? I thought she was inviting me up there."

"Wow. You said no?"

"I don't pay for a woman's company."

"Then you're probably the first one she asked, and the first one to say no."

"Are there any men who come in just to talk to her?" he asked, wondering if there were other gang members in town.

"Plenty, usually ranch hands come in after a hard day's work. We all have those."

"I see."

"Where are you from?"

"Out of town," he said. "Thanks for talking to me."

"Hey, thanks for the champagne, honey," she said. "Come back and see me again."

He pushed his empty beer mug away and got to his feet.

"I'll be back," he said, and walked toward the door.

***

Across the room, hidden from view by an assemblage of drinking men standing at the far end of the bar, Stacy watched as Clint Adams walked to the door. She had to find out what he talked with Angela about. Not that the empty headed little blonde knew anything that could hurt them. And in the morning she'd find out what a drunken Mark Crawford had to say to the Gunsmith.

"Champagne, sweet thing?" one of the men asked her.

"Sure, why not?" she said.

"And then one of us will take you upstairs, huh?" another asked.

"Sweetie," she said, with a smile, "not a chance."

***

The walk from the saloon to his rooming house cleared Mark Crawford's head a bit. When he got there he sat on the porch in a wooden chair and tried to remember what he had said to the Gunsmith. Or, what he would have said to the Gunsmith if Stacy hadn't interrupted them.

Stacy was going to be so mad at him tomorrow. He shouldn't have talked to Clint Adams, or even allowed him to sit with him. Now that Adams had a good, close look at his face. How was he going to convince the Gunsmith that he was wrong?

Maybe the thing to do was get rid of him so they could move forward with their plan without him interfering.

But first he needed a good night's sleep.

***

Sheriff Irving was entering his office when he heard a shot ring out in the night, sounding like it was coming right from the center of town.

Goddamn Gunsmith, he thought, and started running.

***

It was a single shot, and even before Clint could take cover, the shooter was gone, having cleanly missed.

Clint turned as he heard someone running up the street, and saw Sheriff Irving coming toward him.

"What the hell, Adams?" he demanded.

"Beats me, Sheriff," Clint said. "Somebody took a shot at me from the dark."

The two men stood in the center of the street, looking around them.

"Do you know from where?"

30

"Not a clue," Clint said. "I was waiting for the muzzle flash from a second shot, but it never came."

"Who did you get mad at you since you got to town?" Irving asked.

"Who knows?" Clint said. "It could've been somebody who recognized me, or knew how much money I got from the bank."

"You're carryin' it around with you?"

"I wasn't about to leave it in my room."

"You ever think about putting it in the bank?"

Clint laughed. "Not that bank."

"Why not?"

"It hires bank robbers as tellers."

"What?"

"Let's go to your office," Clint said. "I got a story to tell you."

Chapter Nine

"Are you sure about this?" Sheriff Irving asked Clint.

"Dead sure," Clint said. "I got a real close look at him tonight. He's older, but it's him."

"Do you know his name?"

"No."

"The name of the gang he was with?"

"No," Clint said. "They all looked too young to be a gang. I had the feeling it was their first job."

"Did you ride with the posse to catch them?"

"No," Clint said. "I was headed out of town when it happened."

"Do you know if the gang was ever caught?"

"No."

"You don't know much, do ya?"

"I know you've got a bank robber working in your bank," Clint said.

"Maybe he robbed a bank ten years ago," Irving said, "but I can't arrest him for that. He might've gone straight, since then."

"And now he works in a bank," Clint said. "What a coincidence."

"What do you want me to do?"

"Talk to him, at least."

"I can do that."

"And talk to a girl over at the River Run named Stacy," Clint added.

"Why her?"

"I get the feeling they know each other," Clint said. "They might have known each other before they came here."

"What makes you think that?"

"I've seen them sitting together."

"That's a saloon girl's job," Irving said, "to sit with the customers."

"And she came over to interrupt us when I was talking with him," Clint added. "He was drunk, and I think I was about to get something out of him."

"Well then," Irving said. "Maybe you should try again."

"Maybe," Clint said. "I'll go and ask him if he took a shot at me."

"Now that," Irving said, "could have nothin' to do with him. How many times have you been shot at in your life?"

"A million," Clint said, "At least."

"Well, you're lucky it was dark," Irving said, "or they were just a bad shot."

"Or," Clint said, "it was just a warning."

"But you don't take warnin's, do ya?"

"Never." Clint stood up.

"That's the one thing I know about all you gunnies," Irving said. "You never back off when you have the chance."

Clint felt that was true about the gunmen—or would-be gunmen—who came after him, but he never thought that about himself. Maybe Sheriff Irving had a point.

"Thanks for your time, Sheriff."

As Clint reached the door Irving said, "I know you don't think much of me as a lawman, Adams. To tell the truth, I don't think much of myself, either. But I'll do what I need to do to keep the job."

"I really don't have an opinion, Sheriff," Clint said. "I'd ride out and leave the whole business to you, if I thought it was the right thing to do."

"But you don't."

"It's what I did ten years ago," Clint said. "Now, maybe it's coming back to haunt me."

"I guess I can understand that," Irving said, "but whatever you decide to do, keep me informed, okay?"

"Agreed, Sheriff."

As Clint Adams left the sheriff's office, Irving sat back in his chair and wondered what trouble was ahead.

***

Outside the office Clint stopped, looked both ways on the street before starting across. He just hoped that whoever it was who took that shot in the dark, they were done for the night.

He walked to his hotel, feeling a bullseye throbbing on his back. As he entered he thought the desk clerk was paying an inordinate amount of attention to him. He walked to the registration desk.

"What's on your mind?" Clint asked.

"Me? Nothin', sir."

"Then why are you staring at me?"

"Me? Starin'? Not me, sir."

"Come on, come on," Clint said to the meek looking clerk. He had slicked down hair and a pair of glasses he'd probably been wearing for 20 years, since he was 15 years old. "Let me have it."

"Well, sir . . . Mr. Adams . . . she said that you said it was all right if I let her into your room."

"So you did?"

"Uh, yessir."

"And she's up there now?"

"Yessir."

"You didn't happen to notice if she had a gun, did you?" Clint asked.

Now the clerk grinned and said, "Not that I could see, sir."

And who was it?"

When the man told him, he could understand why he didn't see a gun.

Chapter Ten

Just because the clerk didn't see a gun didn't mean a thing. She could be waiting in the room with a gunman in tow, or there could be a gunman all alone who she'd let in the back way.

He walked down the hall to his door and listened at it for a moment. There was no conversation going on inside, unless it was in whispers. Just to be on the safe side he put his right hand and on his gun butt, and opened the door with his left.

He let the door swing wide, remaining out in the hallway. She was sitting on his bed, reading a book she had obviously found in his saddlebags. When she looked up she smiled at him. It was a smile he hadn't seen in the saloon.

"I'm impressed by a man who reads," Stacy said, holding the book up and wiggling it. "Especially one who reads Charles Dickens."

He took one step forward, taking a look around the entire room—and behind the door—before entering. Closing the door behind him, he turned to face her.

"And you're a careful man," she added. "I like that, too."

He glanced around the room again, and then took his hand off his gun.

"Thanks for doin' that," Stacy said. "I wasn't sure if you were gonna shoot me or not."

"I guess that all depends on what are you're doing in my room, Stacy."

She looked at the book in her hand, and then set it aside on the bed and forgot it. Leaning back on her hands she crossed her leg and started bobbing it. Her skirt slid up to reveal a silky thigh.

"Well, Mr. Adams—do I have to call you Mr. Adams?"

"Call me Clint."

"Good, Clint. I thought we kinda got off on the wrong foot in the saloon," she said. "So I figured I'd come here and smooth things out."

"What is there to smooth out?" Clint asked. "We agreed that I'm not going to pay you for sex, and you're not going to give it away for free."

"Right," she said, "we did agree to that."

"So?"

"So," she said, getting to her feet and smoothing the front of her green dress, "I thought maybe we should do somethin' about that."

"Like what?"

"Like . . . have sex." She reached behind her to undo her dress.

"Okay, wait a minute," he said, but she didn't. In moments the dress was off crumpled in a corner of the room, followed by some frilly underwear, and she was naked.

She arched her back, which made her round breasts stand out. He could tell they used to be rounder and very hard, but now she was in her 30's and they had acquired a very nice, slightly oblong shape. The curve underneath the nipples looked very sweet and smooth. She ran her hands down her body and smiled at him.

"Why don't we just . . . try it out?" she asked. "Free of charge."

"And then what?"

She shrugged, which made those once hard tits jiggle a bit.

"Then maybe we'll try it again."

"Is this supposed to get my mind off of something else?" he asked.

"Like what?"

"Like asking questions."

"If you want to ask me questions," she said, moving towards him, "why don't you do it . . . after."

"Look," he said, holding his hands up. "I'm not, uh, really all that interested in having sex with you."

As she got closer he could smell a mixture of perfume, girl sweat and sex. It was a heady combination that, combined with the fact she was naked, was having her desired effect on him.

She reached down and pressed her hand to his crotch, feeling the bulge there.

"A part of you sure is," she said, rubbing him through his pants.

"Stacy--"

"Have sex with me," she said, "and then ask me anythin' you want."

She titled her head up and kissed him, this time grabbing hold of his crotch. The kiss went on for some time, her mouth open and her tongue avid. When it was over they were both breathless. She finished it off with a fleeting swipe of that tongue.

"Deal?" she whispered.

The Bank Job

"Deal," he said.

Chapter Eleven

Sex with the Gunsmith was infinitely more enjoyable than sex with Mark Crawford. And it would accomplish more for Stacy.

For one, she wanted to take his mind off of the bank teller, and having his cock in her mouth was doing just that. Secondly, she hadn't had sex since she came to town several months before, and this was really relieving a lot of stress for her.

She wet his hard penis thoroughly with her tongue, and then took it deep into her hot mouth again . . .

***

Clint knew what she was trying to do.

It was obvious to him that she and the bank teller were connected. The question was, did they have any more partners in town—or, perhaps, were waiting for them.

But she was trying to take his mind off of Crawford and, for the moment, she was doing a damn good job of it.

As her head bobbed up and down on him, his cock sliding in and out of her mouth, he reached down to cup her head in his hands.

"Mmmmmm," she moaned, as she sucked him, and he lifted his butt off the bed to drive himself even deeper down her throat. If she did this for a living, he thought, she should be a rich girl.

When he thought she was going to continue to work his prick until it exploded, she allowed him to slide from her mouth, went down beneath his cock to lick his swollen balls, and then slid up his body with a smile until she was stretched out on him, his erection trapped between them.

They kissed, a kiss that went on for a long time, tongues lashing, very wet and hot, as if they each couldn't get enough of the other.

She broke the kiss, then, and peppered his shoulder and chest with kisses, then reached between them to grasp his cock and hold it. She pressed the bulging head to her wet pussy lips and rubbed it there for a few moments—delighting both of them—and then, with a quick thrust of her hips, took him inside. He had been inside many women who were like a steaming cauldron, but Stacy's pussy was simply warm as it closed around him.

She sat straight up on him, wiggling her hips, pressing her hands down flat on his abdomen, leaning and starting to ride him up and down.

Clint kept his eyes open so he could watch her breasts bob, her skin dapple with sweat, the cords on her neck stretch as she allowed her head to loll back as she gave herself up to the sensations riding his cock brought her. She bit her lips, and at one point shook her head to dislodge a drop of sweat that was perched on the end of her nose.

The drop of sweat landed on his lips, and he tasted it with his tongue, and enjoyed it. Her pussy was also gushing liquids, soaking the sheet beneath them. He felt his own sweat adding to the mix. The combined aroma added to the experience rather than detracting from it. He breathed it in deeply, even though he knew they'd both have to take a bath later to get rid of it.

"Oooooh," she growled, "yes, I needed this . . ."

"I thought you did this all the time?" he said.

She stared down at him with an intense look. "Not this, lover. This is special."

He wanted to reply, but at that moment she did something with her insides that seemed to grip him tighter, and he grunted, unable to speak.

"See?" she asked.

He nodded, his own eyes now wide and intense. The woman knew what the hell she was doing!

***

Later, after a mutual explosion left them both gasping for air, they lay side-by-side, catching their breath.

"Sorry about the sheets," she finally said, breathlessly. "I tend to do that when I'm excited."

"Don't worry about it," he said. "I'm flattered."

"You should be," she said. "There's nobody in this town I've wanted to do this with since I got here."

"I hope it was worth it."

"I'll let you know when we're done."

"We're not done?" he asked.

She reached over, grabbed ahold of his cock and said, "Not even close, honey."

She rolled over onto him, got herself situated so she was sitting on his chest, and pressed her pussy up against his face.

No, he thought, they weren't even close to being done . . .

***

Still later, after he had eaten her until she screamed, she slumped down onto him, kissed him deeply, and then slid off to lie next to him again.

"This is gonna sound like boasting," she said, "but I haven't found many men in my life who can keep up with me. You're liable to raise my opinion of them, in general."

"Hey," he said, "don't give any of my credit to anybody else. Let them all earn their own."

"You're right," she said. "You know, I can see now why you don't pay for sex. You don't need to."

"If I was ever tempted," he said, "you could do it."

"I'll take that as a compliment."

"That's how I meant it."

He sat up, pressed his back to the bedpost, causing his gunbelt to swing momentarily.

"You always keep that so close?" she asked.

"Always," he said, "sex, a bath, whatever."

"I guess that happens when so many attempts have been made on your life."

"Including tonight."

She sat up, leaned against him and asked, "You think I'm tryin' to kill you with sex?"

"No," he said, "on the way to the hotel tonight, somebody took a shot at me."

"What? Do you know who it was?"

"No, it was dark. They took one shot, missed, and lit out."

"Why would somebody do that?"

"Well, first because people are always taking shots at me," he said. "It's the price I pay for who I am."

"I suppose."

"And second, to warn me off."

"Off of what?" she asked.

"Well," he said, "I'm thinking about your friend, the bank teller."

"Crawford? Why him?"

"Maybe because he's planning something, and he thinks I might ruin it."

"Planning something . . . like what?"

"A bank job."

"He has a bank job," she said. "I mean, he works in a bank."

"And maybe he's planning on robbing it."

"Why would he do that?"

"Why don't you tell me?"

"How would I—wait a minute," she said. "Do you think I'm involved?"

"Why else would you be here, trying to distract me?"

She got off the bed and glared at him. As she started to get dressed she said, "That's what you think this was?"

"It's not?" he asked.

"You know," she said, dressed and moving toward the door, "maybe being shot at so many times had rattled your brain."

"Hey," he said, "what about our deal?"

"What deal?"

"You said if I had sex with you, I could ask whatever questions I want."

"Oh yeah," she said, "I did say that. But I didn't say I'd answer them!"

She slammed the door on the way out.

Chapter Twelve

He started the next morning with a bath.

The smell of Stacy in the room and on his body was not unpleasant, but he didn't want to carry it around with him all day.

After she stormed out the night before he had smiled at her act of indignation. Her ploy to fuck him into ignorant oblivion had failed. All she had done was convince him even more that he was right about her and bank teller, Crawford, or whatever his real name was. He had rolled over onto her side of the bed—the drier side—and gone to sleep.

In the morning he went down to the lobby, asked the clerk to draw him a hot bath, and to have clean, dry sheets put on his bed.

While he was in the tub, with his gunbelt nearby, he thought about the saloon girl and the bank teller. He doubted that they planned to rob the bank, just the two of them. There had to be more people involved—men or women. And maybe his presence was going to throw their timing off. Hence the warning shot the night before.

He finished his bath, dried off and got dressed. In the lobby he stopped at the front desk, again.

"I'm done," he said.

"Okay," the clerk said, "I'll have the tub drained."

"And my sheets?"

"Already changed, Mr. Adams," the man said. "And I opened the window to . . . air the room out."

"Good idea," Clint said. "I appreciate it."

"Yes, sir. Whatever you want, just let us know."

Clint nodded, crossed the lobby and left the hotel.

***

Mark Crawford woke from a fitful night's sleep. His head ached, and his mouth felt as if hair had grown on his tongue. He got dressed and went downstairs for breakfast.

"You're late," his landlady said.

The dining room table was cleared. Everyone else in the rooming house had eaten and gone.

"I'm sorry," he said. "I'll go out—"

"Sit down," the middle-aged woman said. "I saved somethin' for you."

She went back in the kitchen, came out with a plate and a mug of coffee, set them down in front of him. Then she kissed him on top of the head and sat down next to him. She put her hand in his lap.

"Emma—" he said.

"What? Nobody's around."

"I feel lousy."

She rubbed his crotch, felt him respond. She was about a dozen years older than he was, but the first time she had crept into his room in the dark and got into bed with him, he hadn't complained.

"This is why I like younger man," she said, squeezing him. "Even when they're feelin' lousy, they're ready."

"Emma—"

She undid his pants, got on her knees, and took him into her mouth.

"Jesus . . ."

***

After breakfast she brought him another cup of coffee.

"Feel better?" she asked.

"Yes."

"Why did you come home drunk last night?" she asked. "I waited in bed for you, but . . ."

"I . . . just had a bad day," he said.

She studied him with her lovely, violet eyes. He noticed the lines at the corners of her eyes and mouth. He'd been with older women, before. This time it was so he didn't have to pay rent. Other times it was for money. And he wasn't very inventive in bed, they just liked having a younger man pay attention to them.

"But I make you feel better, don't I?"

Actually, getting serviced by her while he was drinking her coffee did make him feel better, so he said, "Yes, Emma, you do."

"There's my boy," she said, patting his cheek. That part of their relationship he didn't like, being treated like a little boy. If only Stacy was having sex with him, he wouldn't bother with Emma. Maybe soon . . .

"I gotta get dressed for work," he said.

"Wouldn't you like to take the day off and spend it in bed with me?" she asked.

She wasn't bad looking, smelled nice, had pretty skin and many skills. Spending a day in bed with her would have been nice, but he had things to do.

"Maybe tomorrow," he promised.

"Oh well," she said, picking up his cup and kissing him on the cheek, "have a nice day, then."

He went upstairs to get dressed for the bank.

Chapter Thirteen

Clint felt refreshed and hungry as he stepped out of the hotel. Since this was his first morning in town he didn't know where to go for breakfast, so he just started walking. The hotel had a dining room, but the smells wafting from it were not pleasant.

He walked several blocks before he came to a small café with delicious smells coming from it. In his experience, these small places usually had the best food in most towns. This one smelled like it was no exception.

He went inside.

"Sit anywhere," a bored looking man told him. He looked more like a lumberjack than a waiter.

"Why so empty?" he asked. "It smells great in here."

"You missed the breakfast crowd," the man said. "It is after nine, Mister."

"I'll take a table in the back," Clint said.

"Sure you don't want one by the window?"

"I'm sure."

Clint went to a back table and sat. The man followed with a pot of coffee and a cup.

"Coffee?" he asked.

"Definitely."

The man poured the coffee, then stepped back and looked at Clint.

"What're?'

"Oh, nothin' . . ."

"Come on, spit it out."

"Well, you wear that gun like you know how to use it, and you don't wanna sit by the window," he said. "Is my place gonna get shot up?"

"Not if I can help it," Clint said. "I'll just keep a low profile back here."

"Well, okay," the man said. "What can I get ya?"

"How are your steak-and-eggs?"

"Second best in town."

"Second best? Where's the best?"

"Emma Cleary's rooming house, but she only feeds ya if you're stayin' there."

"Well then," Clint said, "this is probably the best I can get."

"Comin' up, Mister."

The man went into the kitchen, and Clint looked around the empty interior. The tables and chairs matched, but they were as old as the peeling wallpaper.

He knew the food would be good.

Chapter Fourteen

"That was excellent," he told the waiter/owner.

"I know," the man said.

"You cooked it?"

"I'm the cook, the waiter, the cleaner," the man said.

"What's your name?"

"Cody," the man said. "Smithers."

"Well, Cody Smithers, my name's Clint Adams."

"I knew it."

"You knew I was Adams?"

"I knew you'd be somebody like the Gunsmith."

"Why don't you sit and have a cup of coffee with me?" Clint asked.

"Why not?" Smithers said. "The breakfast rush is over."

He sat across from Clint, who poured a cup of coffee for him.

"Was there really a breakfast rush?"

"Yes."

"What was it like?"

"A lot like this," Smithers said, sipping the coffee.

"Why is that?"

"Well," Smithers said, "I have a habit of speakin' my mind, and not toin' the line."

"So you're not paying for protection."

"Somethin' like that. What's it to you, Mr. Adams?"

"Call me Clint."

"Okay, Clint."

"There," he said, "now we're friends. I don't like when my friends are mistreated."

Smithers stared at him a few moments, then laughed and poured them both some more coffee.

"What's on your mind, Clint? Just get to town?"

"Yesterday," Clint said. "But I was here last week to talk to the sheriff about some rustlers. Then I left, caught them, and came back."

"Who'd they rustle?"

"The Jameson place."

"Mr. Jameson is one of the few decent men around here," Smithers said. "He's even eaten here a time or two."

"I would've thought he always ate at the Cattleman's Club," Clint said.

"My food is better."

"I've eaten in both places," Clint said, "and you're right."

"So what's on your mind?" Smithers asked, again.

"The Bank of Truxton," Clint said. "What can you tell me about the manager?"

"Winslow?" Smithers asked. "Walks around town with his nose in the air. He's never eaten here. He's on the Town Council."

"Are you on the Council?"

"No."

"But you own a business."

"If you can call it that," Smithers said.

"I do."

"Thanks. So you need help?"

53

"I do," Clint said.

"Well," Smithers said, sitting back and folding his arms, "I've got nothin' better to do."

"You look like a lumberjack," Clint said, "not a cook."

"Actually, I used to be a lumberjack, then I changed to cook. Now I'm a . . . what's the word . . . oh yeah, a restauranteur." Smithers smiled.

"That's a big word."

Smithers frowned. "What, I'm a big guy so I shouldn't know big words?"

"No," Clint said, "I meant it's a new one on me."

"Oh."

"You got any money in that bank?"

"No," Smithers said, "my account is in the other bank. The small one."

"Okay," Clint said. "I saw a teller in the Truxton Bank, recognized him from a bank robbery ten years ago, in Missouri."

"Jesus," Smithers said, "and now he's got a job in a bank?"

"Right."

"He must be plannin' on robbin' it."

"Or he's gone straight."

"And got a job in a bank?" Smithers asked. "That's too much of a coincidence."

"That's what I thought. Do you know any of the girls who work in the saloons?"

"No," Smithers said. "I mean, once in a while, but I don't know any of them."

"What about a girl named Stacy? At the River Run?"

"No. What's she got to do with it?"

"She's new in town, he's new in town," Clint said. "I think they know each other."

"So she's a bank robber, too?"

"I don't know," Clint said. "He's the only one I saw back then."

"So if he has partners, you won't know them."

"No."

"Tell me," Smithers said, "why do you care? If anythin', you're more new in town than they are. What does it matter what they do after you leave?"

"The sheriff asked me the same question. I don't know what this fellow has done since I saw him in Missouri, but I rode out of town that day. Maybe if I'd ridden with the posse instead, I wouldn't be faced with this dilemma now. So one way or another, I'd like to finish this."

"I guess that makes sense," Smithers said. "What do you want from me?"

"Just information," Clint said. "On Winslow, or on whoever owns that River Run . . ."

"That'd be Cade Dillon," Smithers said. "What are you thinkin', that Winslow and Dillon have knowingly hired bank robbers?"

"I don't know," Clint said. "Would they?"

"I doubt it," Smithers said. "Winslow's been the bank manager for ten years, and Cade's owned the River Run since I opened a dozen years ago."

"So they're well established in this town."

"Very well established."

"Have you heard about either of them having money problems?" Clint asked. "Maybe some rumors?"

"Not a word," Smithers said. "And I hear people talkin' about things in here all the time. They tend to forget that while I'm servin' them food, I can also hear 'em."

"I guess that's the case in most restaurants," Clint said. "I'm going to be in town a while, over at the Truxton House. If you think of anything that might help me, I'd appreciate hearing about it."

"I probably won't," Smithers said, "but if I hear anything, I'll let ya know."

"I appreciate it," Clint said. "What do I owe you for the meal?"

"A dollar."

"Worth more," Clint said.

"A dollar'll do it."

Clint paid Smithers and left the café.

Chapter Fifteen

Stacy went into the Truxton Bank that afternoon, saw Mark Crawford behind his cage, doing his job. He was waiting on a woman who had a 5 or 6-year-old boy tugging on her skirts.

"Now, cut that out, Willie Ames!" she scolded him.

"Aw, Ma, I wanna go."

"We'll go as soon as I finish my business here, now cut that out!"

"Aw, Ma . . ."

Stacy waited for Mrs. Ames to finish her business and leave with Willie before approaching the cage.

"Hello, Mark."

Mark looked up from the money he was counting and brightened when he saw her.

"Stacy!" Then he frowned. "Whataya doin' here?"

"I thought you might wanna go to lunch."

Mark looked at the clock on the wall, saw that it was almost noon.

"Yeah, I guess I could go now." He looked at the faded looking, middle-aged woman in the cage next to him. "Tilly, would you tell Mr. Winslow I went to lunch?"

"Sure, Mark." She looked at Stacy and sniffed audibly.

He came around from behind the counter and left the bank with Stacy.

She picked the place to eat, a small café a few blocks from the bank, off the main street. The place was small, with a half dozen or so tables, only one of which was taken.

"Take a table," the waiter said.

"Over there," she said to Mark, "away from the window."

"Sure," Mark said. "I'd prefer Emma didn't see us eatin' together."

"You and Emma, huh?" Stacy said.

"Why not?" Mark said, as they sat. "She's a nice woman."

"A little old, ain't she?"

"I've been with older," Mark said.

"Is that somethin' to brag about?" she asked.

"Just fact. Older women usually have more money."

"And you go after them."

"I didn't go after her," Mark said. "She came to the bank, saw me, and she come after me."

"Well, why not?" Stacy asked. "You're a good lookin' young fella."

"Not good-lookin' for you, though, huh?"

"Aw, Mark . . ."

"Never mind," Mark said. "What's this about? Bein' seen with me in public?"

"This ain't public," she said. "And we needed to talk while you're still sober."

The waiter came over and they both ordered sandwiches.

"I'm sorry about last night," Mark said to her. "I didn't mean to get drunk and talk to Adams."

"Do you remember what you said to him?"

He rubbed the back of his neck. "Not all of it."

"That's too bad."

"We gonna give up our plan?"

"Hell, no," she said. "All we've got to do is wait. Adams will ride out, and the rest of 'em will get here."

"You really think so?"

She nodded. "I really think so. Besides, we've got Winslow in place. You know how long it would take us to go to another town, find another bank manager we can turn? No, we ain't leavin', Mark, and we ain't changin' our plans."

"What about Adams?"

"I told you," she said. "He'll ride out. We just need to sit and wait."

"And if he don't?"

"Then when the rest of the boys get here," she said, "we'll take care of him."

"You think the boys'll like the idea of goin' up against the Gunsmith?"

"Are you kiddin'?" she asked. "They'll love it!"

Chapter Sixteen

After lunch they left the café separately. Stacy admitted to herself that it might have been a mistake for them to go to lunch together.

"Let's go back to the way it was," she told him. "We'll only talk in the saloon."

"Okay," Mark agreed.

"And don't talk to Adams again, understand?"

"I got it," Mark said. "But what if he comes lookin' for me?"

"Mark," she said, "no matter what he says, just keep denyin' it. You ain't a bank robber, understand?"

"Sure, Stacy, I understand."

She let him leave the café first, gave him about five minutes, then walked out. Only the waiter and people at the other table had seen them—and Tilly, the teller in the bank. People on the street hadn't paid them any mind.

Her plan was still in place.

***

Clint went to the bank, looking for Mark Crawford. He wanted to give the younger man another shove. Instead, he talked to Tilly.

"He left with that hussy from the saloon," she told him, sniffing loudly. "Don't know what a nice young man like him would be doin' with a gal like that one."

"Which one, Ma'am?" Clint asked. "Do you know her name?"

"I didn't, but Mark said her name. It was Stacy."

"Thank you."

"If you don't find him," she said, "you might look in at Emma Cleary's rooming house. He's got a room there."

"Thank you kindly, Ma'am." He tipped his hat and left.

***

When he got to the rooming house he knocked on the front door. It was opened by a handsome woman in her forties, wearing a simple blue dress, with a white apron over it. She had her dark hair pulled back, but some tendrils had come loose while she'd been cleaning, and were hanging down over her face.

"Yeah?" she asked, blowing the hair away momentarily.

"I'm sorry to bother you while you're busy, but I'm look-ing for Mark Crawford, Ma'am," he said. "Does he have a room here?"

"He does," she said. This time she swept the hair out of her face with the back of her hand. "Why do you need him?"

"Oh, we just have some business," he said.

"Did you check the bank, where he works?"

"I did. He wasn't there. A lady teller told me he left with a woman."

Emma Cleary's eyes flared, and Clint noticed.

"What woman?"

"Oh, she said it was a girl from the saloon," Clint said. "Her name was . . . Stacy, I think?"

"That hussy!"

"That's what the lady teller called her."

"That'd be Tilly," Emma said. "She and I have a lot of the same opinions of people in this town."

"I see."

Emma seemed to make an effort to regain control of her temper, and succeeded.

"Well, what's your name, Mister? I'll tell Mark you were here lookin' for him."

"Now, I'd appreciate that, Miss . . . Cleary, is it?"

"Just call me Emma," she said. "Everybody does."

"Wait," Clint said. "You're the Emma Cleary who's such a good cook?"

She brightened.

"You heard about me?"

"I did. I had a steak in a café, fellow told me I was having the second-best steak in town. Told me you made the best."

"I do pride myself on my cookin'," she said.

"He told me you only cook for your guests," Clint said. "Too bad I'm staying at the Truxton House."

"That's a fine hotel," she said, "but their dining room ain't that good."

"I could tell that from the smell," he admitted.

"I tell you what," she said. "Since you're a friend of Mark's, why don't you come by for supper tonight?"

"Well, that's very nice of you."

"A few of my guests don't get off work til five, so I serve supper at six sharp."

"I'll be here at one minute til," he promised. "I don't want to miss it."

"There'll be a seat at my table for you, Mr. . . . you never did tell me your name."

"It's Clint Adams."

"Well, there'll be a seat for you, Mr. Adams. Right next to Mark."

"Why don't we make that across from him," Clint said. "I wouldn't want him to miss seeing me."

"That's a good idea, Mr. Adams—"

"Just call me Clint."

"I'll see you at six, Clint."

He held up his index finger and said, "One minute til."

Chapter Seventeen

He had almost turned down the invitation to supper, but then reconsidered for two reasons:

First, he really wanted to taste Emma Cleary's cooking;

Second, it would put some pressure on Mark Crawford to see him at the table.

He went back to the hotel, spent the rest of the day sitting in a chair in front of the building, watching the town go by. He thought about looking for Stacy and Mark. Catching them together, but then decided against it. He wanted the next time Crawford saw him to be at Emma Cleary's table.

While he sat there, watching, he tried to figure out Stacy and Crawford's plan. If they had one, they probably would have done it, already. That meant there were more players involved, and they were probably waiting for them to arrive. The two had come ahead to establish themselves, and get things ready.

Did establishing themselves also mean getting the bank manager involved? The man had been in that position for ten years. Why would he now be part of a plot to rob his bank? Winslow needed a little closer looking at.

But first, supper with Mark Crawford.

***

When Emma Cleary opened the door and saw Clint Adams there she said, "One minute to six. Right on time."

"Thank you again for the invitation."

She walked him into the dining room, introduced him as Clint, a guest for supper. She then reeled off the names of the five others seated there, all men, of varying sizes and ages.

"Where's Crawford?" he asked her.

"He always comes down late," she said.

"Good," he said. He'd be sitting there in a very good position to see the expression on the teller's face when he saw Clint.

He sat down between a bored looking man in his 40's on his left, and a sleepy looking man in his 50's on his right.

"Jack Gregory," the man on his left said. "Drummer, ladies unmentionables."

"Clint," he said, and they shook hands.

"Ted Dorsey," the man on his right said, "I'm an advisor, here to meet with the mayor and town council to advise them on ways to strengthen the town infrastructure."

"Clint," he said, and shook hands.

"You didn't say why you're here," Dorsey commented.

"Just passing through," Clint said. "I heard Emma was the best cook in town, and it smells like I heard right."

"I thought she only fed guests," Gregory said.

"I am a guest," Clint said. "Hers."

"Ah . . ." Gregory said, nodding because he thought he knew what that meant.

As Emma started bringing out platters of food and putting them on the table, Mark Crawford came down the stairs.

"Sorry I'm late . . ." he was saying.

"As usual," Dorsey muttered.

He hurried to his place, seated himself and then saw Clint sitting across from him and froze.

"Hello, Mark," Clint said.

"What are you doin' here?" Crawford asked.

"I'm a guest," Clint said.

"You're stayin' here?"

"No," Clint said, "I'm just Emma's guest for supper."

"You know Emma?" Crawford asked.

"I do now," Clint said. "We met this afternoon, when I came here looking for you."

"Why were you looking for me?"

"Everybody start eating!" Emma called out. "Do your yalkin' while you're chewin'."

"Harsh taskmistress," Dorsey said, grabbing some chicken from a platter and then passing it to Clint. "Jack, you give her some of that frilly stuff you got, yet?"

"I tried," Jack said, taking the platter from Clint, "she wasn't havin' any."

"I guess she's too busy with the bank teller," Dorsey said, in a low tone.

"Emma and Mark?" Clint asked him.

"Oh yeah," Jack Gregory said. "Apparently our lovely landlady likes 'em young."

"So she turned you boys down?" Clint asked.

"Flat," Ted Dorsey said.

"Oh yeah," Jack said. "Put me in my place, too."

"I guess she doesn't know that <u>we</u> all know she sneaked into Mark's room the first night he was here."

"How do you know?" Clint asked. "Were you all here, then?"

"No," Jack said, "but the word gets passed on from guest-to-guest."

Clint looked across the table at Mark, who was eating and stealing glances at him.

"As long as he's in her bed," Jack whispered to Clint, "he doesn't pay rent."

"Good deal, if you can get it," Clint observed.

Chapter Eighteen

Smithers was right.

Emma Cleary's food was better than the Cattleman's Club, and better than his. Therefore, she probably was the best cook in town.

After she cleared the table of the remnants of supper, she brought out two different complete pies and cut them into slices. While the men at the table chose their flavors—apple, or peach—she went back to the kitchen for coffee.

"Peach is my favorite," Clint said, anxiously snagging a slice.

"Apple's for me," Jack said.

"Me, too," Ted echoed.

"Good," Clint said, "because I'll probably be wanting a second slice."

He looked across at Mark Crawford, whose appetite seemed to have been affected by something.

"No pie, Mr. Crawford?" Clint asked.

"I'm . . . not hungry, anymore."

Emma came back with the coffee and poured everyone a cup.

"Not for me, Emma," Mark said.

"Nonsense," she said. "Have a cup, and a slice of peach pie. I made it for you."

"Ah, is peach your favorite, Mark?" Clint asked.

"Yes, it is," Emma answered for him.

"Mine, too," Clint said.

"Well, you two look like the only ones," Emma said to Clint, "so eat as much as you like."

"Thank you," he said, already reaching for a second slice.

Crawford looked like he was forcing himself to eat it, to please Emma.

After desert the men left the table to go to their own entertainments. Three headed for a saloon, two went up to their rooms.

"Care to go to the saloon, Clint?" Ted asked, before they left.

"I probably will, in a while. Which one?"

"We both like roulette," Jack said, "so we'll be at the Black Horse."

"Good, I'll see you there," Clint promised.

That left Emma, Mark and Clint in the dining room. When Emma went to the kitchen Mark leaned forward in his chair.

"Why are you here?" he demanded.

"Emma invited me."

"Why were you lookin' for me today?"

"Just to talk."

"I don't wanna talk to you."

"Why not?" Clint asked.

"Because you think I'm a bank robber."

"Aren't you?"

"No!"

"Then weren't you, ten years ago?"

"No!"

"So you're just going to continue to deny it?"

"Yes!" Mark said, then, "No! I mean—there's nothin' to deny."

"Then why are you so . . . worked up?"

"Because I don't like bein' accused of bein' a criminal," Mark said.

"What about Stacy?" Clint asked.

"The saloon girl? What about her?"

"Is she your partner?"

"My Part—what are you talkin' about?"

"The two of you knew each other before you came here, isn't that right?"

"No, it's not." He lowered his voice. "If you make Emma believe that, there's gonna be trouble."

"But you had lunch with her today."

At that moment Emma came out of the kitchen.

"I'm goin' to my room," Mark announced.

"Not going out tonight, Mark?" Emma asked.

"No."

"Then I'll see you later."

He nodded, and quickly went up the stairs.

"What did you do to him that made him run like that?" she asked.

"We just talked."

"About what?"

Clint took a deep breath. "Stacy."

He saw Emma's nostrils flair.

"What about that painted hussy?"

"I have the feeling she and Mark knew each other before they came here."

70

"What makes you think that?"

"I saw them together in the saloon last night," he said. "And today they had lunch together."

"Why would he have lunch with her?"

"To decide what to do," he said, "about me."

"I don't understand."

"I think," Clint said, "they're planning to rob the Truxton bank."

"Why would Mark rob the bank he's working for?"

"That may be why he took the job," Clint said.

She stared at the stairway leading up to the second floor. "I don't believe it." She turned and looked at him. "Can you prove that?"

"Not yet," he said "but I'm working on it."

"I think you better go."

Chapter Nineteen

Clint found both Jack and Ted at the roulette table in the Black Horse Saloon.

"There you are!" Ted Dorsey exclaimed. "I'm up a hundred dollars."

"That's good."

"Did anyone come with you?" Jack Gregory asked, looking behind him.

"No," Clint said. "Just me."

Jack and Ted exchanged a look.

"I bet I know what Mark and Emma are doin', right now," Jack said.

"You never know," Clint said. "You might be wrong."

"I don't think so," Ted said. "That woman—according to the last young stud she had in her house—can't be satisfied. That's why she picks young men."

"Well," Jack said, "we ain't so old that we wouldn't be able to do it, if she gave us the chance."

"Which she ain't," Ted said. "You playin' fifteen again, Jack?"

"You know it."

"I'm stickin' with twenty-four!" Ted said. He looked at Clint. "It's come up twice, already."

"Is that so?" Clint asked.

"You better get on it," Ted said.

The wheel spun.

"Come on, fifteen!" Ted shouted.

Clint quickly bought some chips, and went ahead and played 24.

"Oh yeah!" Ted yelled, as the small ball started bouncing about on the wheel—and came to a stop on 24.

"Damn!" Jack snapped.

"Oh yeah!" Ted yelled, again.

***

Emma opened the door to Mark's room and entered.

"Not now, Emma," he said, expecting her to be naked. He was surprised to see she was fully dressed.

"Are you a bank robber?" she asked him.

"What?"

"Are you planning to rob your bank?"

"Of course not," he said. "You should know me better than that."

"I don't know you at all, Mark," she said. "You live here, and we sleep together. That's all I know."

"Well, I'm tellin' you," Mark said, "I'm not a bank robber. I don't know what Clint Adams is tryin' to pull."

"Was he tellin' the truth about you and that girl, Stacy?" she asked.

"What did he say?"

"That you knew each other before you came here."

"No," he said. "I met Stacy around the same time I met you, Emma."

"So you had lunch with her today?"

73

Mark stared at Emma, unsure what to say. How was he supposed to explain?

"Is that hussy chasin' you?" Emma asked. "Is that it?"

"Yes," he said, "yes, that's it. She's chasin' me and I didn't know how to say no. But nothin' happened. We only had lunch."

"You can do whatever you want, Mark," Emma said. "Just remember, you owe me a lot of back rent."

"I do."

Emma started to unbutton her dress and said, "Well, you *could*, start paying me back a little right now."

Mark knew what was coming, so while Emma took off her clothes he turned down the bed. When he looked at her again, she was naked. She was thin, with small, hard breasts and prominent hip bones. Still, she was far from unattractive, with smooth skin, long dark hair that she had unpinned so it flowed down around her shoulders, and lovely eyes—eyes that were filled with lust and need, at that moment.

She approached Mark Crawford, grabbed him, kissed him hard, and then started to undress him quickly. Mark sometimes felt like a ragdoll, the way Emma jerked his clothes from him, but when he was naked her focus went right to his hard cock, and that he didn't mind.

She got down on her knees and gobbled up his penis, then started to suck it, her head bobbing back and forth. Then, still on her knees, she pushed him back until he fell onto the bed.

From there she crawled on top of him and impaled herself on his hard dick. He didn't have the biggest penis, or the hardest she had ever ridden, but he was young, and that was what she enjoyed about Mark Crawford. She knew that hard cock inside of her would stay hard for as long as she wanted it to, until she was done with it.

"This is where you forget about that hussy, Stacy," she told him, riding him up and down, grinding every time she came down, "Because this is where you belong, boy, for as long as I want you."

Chapter Twenty

"You know," Emma said, as she slipped her dress back on, "I really don't care."

"Wha—" Mark said. He was still out of breath, for she had ridden him hard and long before allowing him to explode inside her.

She went and sat on the bed, reached over and took his limp penis in her hand. As she stroked it, it began to get hard again, as she knew it would.

"You robbin' that bank," she said. "I don't care if that's what you're plannin'."

"Wha—whataya talkin' about?"

"I don't like that bank manager Winslow, and I don't like that bank," she said. "So if you're plannin' on robbin' it, I wish you luck." She tightened her hold on his cock and he tensed. "Even if you're workin' with that cheap saloon girl. Just remember who takes care of this tallywacker." She stroked it until it got good and hard, and then she laughed and slapped it a few times.

"It's mine!" she said, and left the room.

Mark put his hand over his eyes and said, "Jesus!"

***

24 came up two more times, and then suddenly the wheel shifted and 15 came up twice.

Clint rode along with Jack and Ted, and quit when it looked like the wheel was changing, again.

"Come on," he said to the two men, "I'm, buying. You guys just made me some money."

They walked to the bar, which was crowded, and elbowed some room.

"Beer?" Clint asked

Both men agreed. Clint waved at the bartender and ordered three beers.

"Are you fellas always that lucky at roulette?" he asked, handing them their beers.

"Yep," Jack said.

"Well," Ted said, "since we met."

"He's right," Jack said. "Since we started playin' together, we've both been winnin'."

"Why do you think that is?" Clint asked.

"unlucky in love . . ." Jack said.

". . . lucky at . . . roulette?"

Both men laughed.

"That could be," Clint said.

"Do you gamble?" Ted asked.

"I play poker."

"Well?" Ted asked.

"If I do say so myself, yes."

Jack and Ted looked at each other.

"They have a back room game here," Jack said.

"We haven't been able to get into it," Ted said.

"But if you can," Jack went on, "we'll back you."

"What makes you think I could get into the game if you can't?"

"Well," Ted said, "you are Clint Adams, the Gunsmith, right?"

At the supper table he had only told them his name was Clint.

"How do you know that?"

"I travel a lot for my business," Jack said, "and I've seen you before."

"When he told me who you were," Ted said, "I got the idea. Our money, and your talent."

"Not interested," Clint said. "I've got something else going on."

"It only takes one night," Jack said.

"Yeah, you could clean them out in one night, couldn't you?" Ted asked.

"If I was you gents," Clint said, "I'd stick to roulette."

"Roulette is all luck," Jack pointed out.

"And luck runs out," Ted said.

"But poker is a game of skill," Jack said.

"Sorry," Clint said, "my skills are being used for something else, this week."

Jack and Ted exchanged a glance.

"Okay, then," Jack said.

"How about next week?" Ted asked.

Clint watched the two men lose some money at the roulette table, while keeping his own winnings in his pocket. There were a couple of girls working the floor, serving drinks, but they weren't dressed provocatively here, and they didn't have to avoid the groping hands of customers, because the customers were gambling. For men who wanted to gawk at girls, there was the River Run Saloon.

"We're headin' back to the house," Jack said to Clint.

"Finished gambling?"

"The luck is gone," Ted said.

"And we gotta get up early for work tomorrow," Jack added.

"Well, thanks for my winnings," Clint said, patting his pockets.

"You know when to quit, huh?" Jack asked. "That's the secret."

Jack and Ted left, and Clint thought about whether he really knew when to quit?

Chapter Twenty-One

Instead of going back to his hotel, Clint decided to stop into the River Run for one last beer. Also, for the same reason he had gone to Emma Cleary's for supper. He wanted Stacy to see him there, and wonder why?

As he entered he found it busy as the Black Horse Saloon, with the bar crowded elbow-to-elbow. He was about to walk to it, to make room for himself, when someone sidled up alongside him.

"So, you're back."

He looked at the blonde saloon girl.

"Hello, Angela."

She smiled. "You remembered my name."

"Of course," he said. "Why would I forget such a pretty girl's name?"

She looked pleased by the compliment.

"Were you thinkin' of goin' to the bar?"

"I was," he said. "Why?"

"Because I can get you a table."

"Where?"

"Where else?" she asked. "All the way in the back, against the wall."

"Lead on."

He followed the pretty blonde through the crowd, all the while looking for but not spotting Stacy.

"Is Stacy around?" he asked, as he sat.

"Now why are you askin' about her when you got me here?" she demanded, good-naturedly.

"I'll tell you a secret," he said. "We don't like each other, so I think it would annoy her to see me sitting here."

"Well," Angela said, "I'm for anythin' that will annoy that . . . woman. I'll make sure she sees you. Now, what can I get you?"

"A cold beer."

"Comin' up, handsome."

She melted into the crowd and made her way to the bar. Around him men were being rowdy, drinking and arguing and grabbing for the girls as they worked the floor. No one seemed to be paying any special attention to him, but he knew it was very possible that whoever had taken that shot at him was in the crowd.

He expected to see Angela come back through the crush of men with his beer, but instead the person who appeared was the sheriff.

"Sheriff," Clint said, as the man reached his table. "What brings you here?"

"Makin' my rounds," Sheriff Irving said, "and I suddenly got the urge for a beer. Then I saw you back here. Mind if I sit?"

"Not at all," Clint said. "I've got a beer coming, but I'm sure the girl will go back and get you one."

"Not a problem," Irving said.

And Clint saw why. When Angela appeared she was carrying two frosty mugs of beer.

"Here you go, Sheriff," she said setting both beers down.

"Thanks, Angela." He picked his up and drank from it. "I caught her on her way to the bar."

"Uh-huh," Clint said, wondering if Angela had deliberately put him at this table for the sheriff to find. "What's on your mind, Sheriff?"

"I talked to some of the merchants about the shooting," he said. "I thought maybe somebody might have seen somethin' when they opened for business that would indicate the shooter was in there."

"And?"

"Nothin'."

"Well, thanks for trying."

"You haven't come across anybody who mighta done it, have ya?"

"Not one," Clint said. "I'm still looking into Crawford, the bank teller, but I don't have any indication that he might've taken the shot."

The sheriff drank his beer down and stood up. "If I see anybody in town I think is huntin' for a reputation, I'll let you know."

"I'd appreciate that, Sheriff," Clint said, "and watch your own back out there. Apparently, you've got at least one person in town who's a bushwhacker."

"I'll watch it," Irving said, and disappeared into the crowd.

Clint worked his beer down til there was about an inch left when Stacy finally appeared, looking surprised to see him. She was wearing a low cut green gown that showed off the swollen tops of her breasts.

"Well, well," she said, "Angela was right. There you are."

"Here I am."

"I didn't think you'd be able to walk yet."

"It's the other way around," he told her. "I'm energized. What about you?"

She sat across from him.

"Well, I needed a man for one night and you filled the bill," she said. "So I'm good."

"What about my questions?"

"What questions?"

"Remember, you said if we had sex I could ask you some questions."

"Yeah, but I never said I'd answer them, did I?"

"No, you didn't," Clint admitted, "but I'm going to ask them anyway."

"Fine," she said, folding her arm so he couldn't see the tops of her breasts anymore.

"Did you and the bank teller, Mark, know each other before you came here?"

"No," she said. "I came here, then some time later he came, and we met. What am I sayin', we met the way I've met all these men in the saloon."

"So what was lunch about, yesterday?"

She made a face, and he knew that she knew lunch had been a mistake.

"That was your fault," she said.

"What? Me?"

"You awakened somethin' in me when we went to bed," she said. "But I didn't want to come back to you for more, so I went lookin' elsewhere."

He didn't believe that for a minute.

She stood up. "I've got to go to work."

Chapter Twenty-Two

He left the saloon and walked back to his hotel, this time keeping to the shadows, so no one could take a shot at him.

When he got to his room he hung his gunbelt on the bedpost and removed his boots. That was as far as he was going to go, just in case the bushwhacker decided to get a little closer.

When he went to sleep, he was still fully clothed. He'd jammed a wooden chair beneath the doorknob, and placed the pitcher-and-basin on the windowsill as a warning system. Anybody trying to get in through the window would cause a racket.

He drifted off to sleep, still wishing he'd ridden with that posse ten years ago. Then he wouldn't be here . . .

***

The next morning two men rode in, having camped just outside of town the night before so they could ride in early, in daylight. They reined in their horses across from the Truxton Bank, which hadn't opened for business, yet.

"That's it," Jeff Merritt said.

"Why don't we just go in there right now, before it opens, and clean it out?" Dan Felton said. "Nobody's there, and there's hardly anybody on the street."

"Because there's a plan in place, that's why," Merritt said. "Been in place for months. We ain't gonna waste all that plannin'."

"A two way split don't appeal to you?" Felton asked.

"Sure it does," Merritt said, "but maybe after. For now, let's just stick to the plan."

"A plan made by a woman," Felton spat.

"A smart woman."

"Yeah, right."

"Let's find a cheap hotel," Merritt said, "and then take care of the horses."

"And then a saloon?"

"It's early," Merritt said. "We'll hit a saloon as soon as it opens."

"Yeah, okay."

They rode on.

***

Clint came down that morning, gave the dining room a quick sniff. Since it didn't smell too bad today, he went in to have breakfast.

"What was that smell yesterday?" he asked the waiter.

The pleasant looking man in his 30's smiled and said, "That was the new cook, tryin' to do somethin' different with cheese."

"Not today?"

"He got fired," the waiter said. "Today it's just ham-and-eggs or flapjacks."

"I'll take both," Clint said.

"Yessir."

The food wasn't bad. It didn't match what he had at Smithers' café, and it sure didn't match Emma Cleary's, but it was edible, and convenient.

Clint decided that Stacy wasn't going to push easily. She was a smart girl, had guts, and he got the feeling she was in charge. That meant he had to work on Crawford, more. The man didn't have the strength the woman did.

Clint also didn't have any idea how many others were involved. He was hoping to ruin whatever plan they had in effect before the rest of the gang arrived.

And, of course, there was always the possibility that he was totally wrong, that Mark Crawford was just a bank teller, and Stacy was just a saloon girl. But Clint could count on the fingers of one hand the times he had been wrong about something like this. He usually went with his instincts, and they told him that there was a bank robbery already being planned—maybe even already in progress.

Chapter Twenty-Three

When Clint came out of the hotel he saw Dave Jameson crossing the street toward him.

"I was coming to see you," Jameson said.

"I just finished breakfast."

"How about a drink?"

"This early?" Clint asked. "What saloon is open this early?"

Jameson laughed. "The Cattleman's Club. Come on."

Clint walked with Jameson to the Club, where the rancher opened the front door with a key.

"It's empty," he said, once inside, "but we'll serve ourselves."

Before long they were seated in one of the rooms in leather armchairs, with a bottle of whiskey between them.

"How are you comin' with this bank robber of yours?" Jameson asked.

"He denies it, of course, but I'm pretty sure that's why he's here, and there's more . . ." Clint went on to tell Jameson about Stacy.

"So you think a saloon girl is in charge?"

"I do."

"That's odd."

"She strikes me as a smart girl," Clint said.

"Stacy, huh?" Jameson repeated. "I don't know 'er."

"I think she's managing to keep a pretty low profile," Clint said, "not taking any men upstairs with her."

"So when do you think this is gonna happen?" Jameson asked.

"I think they're waiting for more men," Clint said. "Considering they've probably been setting it up for months, who knows?"

"And you're willing to wait?"

"Well," Clint said, "I'm willing to push. What about you? You said you were going to talk to the bank manager."

"I did," Jameson said. "Winslow pretty much told me to mind my own business."

"But you and he don't like each other, right?"

"Right."

"What about the mayor and the town council?" Clint asked. "Can you talk to them?"

"Winslow holds papers on all their loans," Jameson said. "They're not about to shake the tree."

"What do you think, at this point?" Clint asked. "Would Winslow hire an ex-bank robber to work in his bank?"

"Not knowingly."

"Unless . . ."

"Unless what?"

"Unless he's in on it," Clint said.

Jameson sighed. "I know you're thinkin' that, but he's been the manager of that bank for a long time."

"Maybe he's fed up. Is he married?"

"No."

"Then maybe he's under Stacy's influence."

"You think she's controllin' him with sex?" Jameson asked. "Winslow?"

"It's possible."

"Winslow," Jameson said, again, shaking his head. "Have you even seen her near him?"

"No," Clint said, "but I've been watching the bank teller. Maybe I should be watching the bank manager, too."

"Or maybe," Jameson said, "you should be talkin' to Tilly."

"Tilly?"

"Tilly Kenner," Jameson said. "She's been a teller in that bank for a long time. She might know somethin'."

"Okay, then," Clint said, "I'll talk to Tilly, and then I'll keep an eye on Winslow and see what he does after hours."

"What can I do?"

"You've done what you can, I guess," Clint said.

"Well," Jameson said, "just gimme a holler if you need back-up."

They stood up, left the bottle and glasses where they were, and walked out of the Club, Jameson locking up after them.

***

Clint went from the Cattleman's Club to the Truxton Bank, which was just opening for business. He peered in the window, saw Mark Crawford behind his cage, getting ready for the day. Next to him, behind another cage, was an older woman, who he assumed was Tilly, since the third teller's cage was empty.

He liked the idea of approaching Tilly—who he now re-membered talking to once before—right in front of Crawford. The man would have to wonder what it was about.

Clint entered the bank, looked around, saw that he was the only customer present.

As he approached Tilly's cage, Mark Crawford looked up and saw him.

"Oh, what do you want no—" he started to ask, but then saw Clint bypass him and go to the next station. He frowned.

As he reached Tilly's cage she looked up and smiled at him. It took years off her age, that smile. He would have guessed her around fifty, with wire-framed glasses and her hair worn in a bun.

"Oh, hello."

"Good-morning," he said. "Are you Tilly Kenner?"

"Yes, I am," she said. "Can I help you?"

"You can," he said.

"How?"

He smiled broadly. "You can allow me to buy you lunch today."

Chapter Twenty-Four

"It's been a long time since a handsome young man has invited me to lunch."

Clint thought it odd for her to refer to him as a "young" man, since she was probably only about ten years older than he was. He could see she had been an attractive young woman, as she was still appealing in a matronly way. Her hair, once honey-colored, was now shot through with gray, and worn in that tight bun.

"And I've never eaten here," she went on, looking around.

He had taken her to Cody Smithers café.

"I'm sure you'll enjoy the food," he said.

"I trust you're correct."

After they had ordered and she tasted the food, she said, "You're right. The food is delicious."

"I have to confess," he said, "I brought you here under false pretenses."

"Really?" she asked. "Should I be . . . flattered?"

"I just hope you won't be angry," he said, "but I'm interested in some of the people who work at the bank."

"Oh? Like who?"

"Well, Mark Crawford, for one."

"A nice young man," she said.

"How long has he worked at the bank?"

"Only a couple of months."

"And how long have you worked there?"

"Oh, more than ten years."

"So you were there even before Mr. Winslow?"

"That's right."

"And what about Winslow?" Clint asked. "What kind of man is he?"

"He's . . . odd," Tilly said.

"Odd? In what way?"

"He's never been married," she said. "I've never even seen him with a woman."

"Men?"

"Oh heavens, no," she said. "It's just not something he's interested in."

"What is he interested in, then?"

"The bank," she said. "He's often in his office until after dark."

"And he lives alone?"

"Yes."

"Where does he eat?"

"I can't say," she said. "I know he often eats at home, meals he prepares for himself. I'm sure he eats in restaurants every so often, but since I eat at home, I've never seen him."

"And do you live alone, Tilly?"

"I do," she said, "and I cook my own meals. But it's not odd for a woman to do those things, especially not a spinster."

"You've never been married?"

"No, never."

"Why not?" he asked. "You're an attractive woman."

"Western men are . . . brutes," she said, wrinkling her nose.

"What about Eastern men? Why not move east?"

She sighed. "Oh, that's a decision I should have made long ago, but I hadn't yet decided there were no men here worthy of my time. Now, of course, it's too late."

"Why? You're still an attractive woman."

She smiled at him. "Aren't you sweet? I'm a spinster, Mr. Adams. Everybody knows that. Spinsters live and die alone."

"Tilly," he said, "why don't you just give new meaning to the word?"

"Well now," she said, "there's something that has never occurred to me." She leaned forward and stared into his eyes. "How do you suggest I do that?"

He shrugged. "Do things that spinsters don't usually do."

Now she smiled broadly. "Like what? Have sex?"

That surprised him.

"Come now, Mr. Adams," she said, "I may be a spinster, but I never said I was a prude."

"More tea?" he asked her.

***

He walked Tilly back to the bank. Actually, they strolled, and she linked an arm through his left one.

"I am a very good cook, you know," she said.

"Are you?"

"Yes, indeed. You should come to my home for supper one night."

He didn't know why, but he had a feeling he hadn't gotten all he could from her.

"Is that a general statement, or are you inviting me?" he asked.

"I'm inviting you," she said. "Tonight? At seven?"

"I'll be there," he promised.

They reached the front of the bank and stopped. She glanced around at the people passing by, some of whom were looking at them curiously.

"I think this little lunch of ours has already changed the way people are looking at me."

"Good," he said.

"Thank you, Mr. Adams."

"Just call me Clint, Tilly," he said. "I'll see you at seven."

Chapter Twenty-Five

Clint had the feeling that Tilly invited him to supper because she had something else to tell him, and preferred to tell him about it in the confines of her own home.

The question was, what to do with the rest of the day?

***

Merritt and Felton, having checked into a small, cheap hotel at the southern tip of town had taken a couple of hours to rest. Then they walked back toward the center of town in search of a saloon.

"That one," Merritt said, pointing at the Black Horse.

"Didn't that telegram from Stacy say she was workin' at the River Run Saloon?" Felton asked.

"Right," Merritt said, "but we're stayin' away from there, for the time bein'. Right now I just want a cold beer."

"Same here."

The saloon had just opened, so they were the only two customers.

"Step up to the bar, gents," the bartender shouted. "Have a proper lunch!"

"Two beers," Merritt said. "You're open pretty early."

"Biggest saloon in town," the bartender said. "And we open earlier and close later than any other." He set a beer in front of each of them.

"Thanks," Merritt said.

They both picked up their mugs and looked around. The gaming tables were covered, and wouldn't be open until later in the day.

"Why didn't Stacy get a job here?" Felton wondered.

"I think it was easier for her to get the job at the River Run," Merritt said. "All she needed to be was beautiful."

"I'm sure there are pretty girls workin' here," Felton said.

"You want girls, you gotta go to the River Run," the bartender said. "Here you get gamblin', and drinkin.'"

"That suits me," Merritt said.

"That's because you've got Stacy," Felton said.

Merritt was a handsome man who did very well with women, while Felton was a gawky fellow who paid for his pleasures.

"I'm sure she'll be happy to see you, Jeff," Felton went on.

"And I'm sure she'll have a girl or two for you, Dan," Merritt said.

"Plenty of girls over at the River Run for that sort of thing," the bartender said. "Plenty of 'em."

"We'll go and have a look later," Merritt said. "For now, how about some more lunch?"

"Another beer?" the bartender asked.

"No, some food."

"Just go across the street to Smithers," the man said. "He'll feed you well."

"Thanks for the tip," Merritt said.

He and Felton set their empty mugs on the bar and left.

"That must be the place," Felton said, pointing to the small café.

"It doesn't look like much," Merritt said. "Let's take a walk and find a better one."

"Okay," Felton said.

***

Inside Smithers café Clint was eating lunch, in company with only a couple of other occupied tables.

Smithers had been looking out the window, and now looked over at Clint.

"Two strangers just came out of the Black Horse. I thought they were headed over here, but they veered off."

"Strangers?"

Clint got up and walked to the window.

"There." Smithers pointed to two men walking away. "They came out of the Black Horse."

"What makes you say they're strangers?"

"One," Smithers said, "I've never seen them before, and two, I was lookin' out the window when they rode in a few hours ago."

Clint looked at the retreating backs of the two men, again.

"Strangers," he said. "Just what I've been waiting for."

"Why?" Smithers asked, as Clint walked back to his table He and waved at Smithers to join him.

"What's on your mind?" Smithers asked.

Clint kept his voice down.

The Bank Job

"I've been waiting for some strangers to come to town," he said. "I think they're going to be part of the plan to rob the bank."

"And how do you propose to find out if you're right?" Smithers asked.

"That's the easy part," Clint said. "I'm going to ask them."

"And what's the hard part?"

"Stopping them."

Chapter Twenty-Six

Clint assumed the two strangers would eventually find their way to the River Run Saloon. He intended to check there, but first he had to keep his promise to Tilly, and stop by her house for supper.

She had given him directions and he found a small house among other similar looking houses, set apart from the town by a small road. However, it was close enough that he didn't have to saddle Eclipse, his Darley Arabian, but simply walk.

When he reached the house he knocked on the door. He was shocked when she answered it.

Gone was the faded looking, middle-aged teller, gone were the wire-framed glasses and tight bun. Instead, her hair fell down around her shoulders, and she wore a long flowing dress rather than the buttoned up bank suit from earlier in the day.

"You made it," she said, happily. "Supper's almost ready. Come in."

She led him to a small, well-appointed living room that was just off of an equally neat dining room.

"Have a seat," she said, indicating a sofa and matching armchair. "Would you like a drink?"

"No, that's okay," he said. "I'll wait for supper."

"Good," she said, "I have a bottle of wine for us to share with the casserole."

She went into the kitchen and he rose to look at the table, which was set with what looked like her best silverware and plates.

"Here we go," she said, reentering the dining room carrying a casserole bowl. "Come and get it, as they say around the bunkhouse."

He wondered what she knew about bunkhouses, and what was said there?

He walked to the table and sat while she served the food and poured the wine, then settled down in a chair opposite him.

"Well," she said, "it's been a while since I've done this. I hope it came out all right."

He put some chicken and vegetables into his mouth and said, "It's wonderful."

It wasn't wonderful, didn't match the food he'd had at Smithers, or at the rooming house of Emma Cleary, but it <u>was</u> tasty.

"It's something my mother used to make quite often when I was a little girl."

"Did you grow up here?"

"Oh, yes," she said, "I'm Truxton born and raised, I'm afraid. My father died when I was very young, and my mother got jobs cleaning the houses of some of the ranchers in the area."

Maybe that's where her knowledge of bunkhouse talk came from.

"We lived in a smaller house in town. When she died I stayed there, but once I started working I saved the money to buy this house for myself."

"And you've worked in the bank now for ten years?"

"I thought about that after lunch today," she said. "It's more like a dozen."

"And before that?"

"I cleaned people's homes for a while, as my mother did, then I started clerking in the general store then the millinery, when one opened here in town."

"And no men?"

She stared at him in a bemused way.

"Did I say that?" she asked. "I never married, but that doesn't mean there were no men, Clint. "I may be a spinster, but I'm no blushing virgin."

The way she had referred to Stacy as a "hussy" made him think she was something of a prude, but maybe that wasn't the case. She was certainly attractive enough to have had some men be interested in her, over the years.

They drank more wine while they ate and talked, and when the plates were empty and there was very little casserole left, he broached the subject he had been thinking about.

"Tilly," he said, "after lunch today I had the feeling that there was some more you could have told me."

"Oh? About what?"

"I don't know," he said. "Maybe about the bank, or about Winslow, the manager? Maybe about Mark Crawford?"

"I told you everything I know about Mark," she said. "He's only been there a matter of months, and he keeps to himself."

"And what about Winslow?"

She hesitated then said, "I have cobbler for dessert, and coffee. Why don't we talk further over that?"

"All right. Let me help you clear—"

"No, no," she said, getting to her feet quickly, "you're my guest. Just finish your wine while I clear the table, and come back with the dessert. Then we'll talk some more."

He had the feeling he was about to find out something helpful.

Chapter Twenty-Seven

Tilly Kenner turned out to be a better baker than she was a cook.

"How's the cobbler?" she asked, after he'd taken his first bite.

"It's excellent," he said, and meant it. The apples almost melted in his mouth, and there was just enough cinnamon. The crust was light and flaky, and her coffee was strong and good.

"I had a feeling a man like you would like his coffee strong," she said.

"You've got that right," Clint said. "I'm used to strong trail coffee, and this is great."

"Good," she said, "I'm glad you're enjoying everything."

"I am, thank you," he said. "But now I'd like to talk more."

"Yes," she said, "about the bank? And Nathan Winslow?"

"Exactly."

"Well, the fact is, Nathan wasn't always a bank manager," she told him. "He was a lawyer for a long time, but when he defended a woman he loved and she was sentenced to death, he quit."

"He was in love? He doesn't seem the type."

"He was, once, but he isn't anymore," she said. "Now he keeps to himself and does his job."

"Are you and he friends?"

"No, no," she said, "I'm just one of his employees."

"Tell me, Tilly," Clint asked, "is he a happy man?"

"Happy? No, I don't think he's happy. Not since his woman was executed."

"Do you think he would rob his own bank, if he thought he could get away with it?"

"Rob the bank?" she asked. "What would make you ask me that?"

"I believe there's a plan in play to rob the Truxton bank," he told her. "I'm trying to find out who's going to do it."

"And you think Nathan Winslow is involved?"

"Possibly."

"What would make you think that?"

Clint wasn't sure he should tell Tilly about Mark Crawford. She might not be able to stay there and work next to him if he did. On the other hand, she wasn't the gentle bank teller he originally thought she was.

"Come on, now," she said. "It's just you and me here. Tell me, why do you think he's involved?"

"First answer me this," Clint said. "Did he hire Mark?"

"Yes."

"Did he check his background at all?"

"He sent a telegram," she said, "to the last place Mark said he worked. Why?"

"I recognized Mark the first time I came into the bank," he told her. "Ten years ago I saw him robbing a bank in Missouri."

"And he's working in a bank now?"

"Odd, isn't it?"

"Well, maybe he went on the straight and narrow at some point."

"Maybe," Clint said. "I just find it too much of a coincidence that he has a job in a bank. And there's something else."

"What?"

"I'm sure that Mark knew Stacy before they came to this town."

"But they came here separately," Tilly said.

"Probably the plan, to come here separately, pretend they don't know each other and get themselves jobs."

"My God," Tilly said, "but what does Nathan Winslow have to do with it?"

"That's what I'm trying to figure out."

"And when do they intend to rob the bank?"

"I believe they're waiting for more gang members to arrive," Clint said. "And two strangers rode in today, so after we're finished here, I'm going to look into them."

"After we're finished?"

"Yes."

"And when will that be?"

"Well," he said, looking at the empty pie plates and coffee cups, "I guess we already are. Unless you want me to help you clear?"

"Yes," she said. "I think I would like you to help me clear the table."

"Okay."

"I'll carry mine into the kitchen, and you carry yours."

"Sounds fair," he said, wondering why she hadn't wanted help with the bigger job of clearing away the supper remnants?

They both stood up, picked up their plate, fork and cup, and he followed her into the kitchen.

It was small and somewhat cramped with both of them in there. She placed her plate and cup by the sink, and then he reached around her to do the same. When he straightened, she was directly in front of him, almost in his arms, staring up at his face.

"I told you I wasn't a prude, didn't I?" she asked.

"Yes, you did."

She pressed her body to his, tilted her head up and kissed him.

"I don't think we're going to be finished here for a while," she whispered.

Chapter Twenty-Eight

In total surprise Clint allowed Tilly to lead him by the hand to her bedroom. There she disrobed, showing him her surprisingly lean, taut body. She closed her eyes and ran her own hands over her breasts and nipples, down her abdomen until they were between her legs.

Definitely not a prude, he thought, as his cock swelled. Even if she was 50 years old, she was an incredibly sensuous and sexy woman.

She opened her eyes and moved to him, started to undo his gunbelt. He gently pushed her hands away, undid it himself and set it close by the bed. After that he let her undress him, which she did slowly.

She removed his shirt, ran her hands over his chest and peppered it with light kisses. Then she pushed him down into a seated position on the edge of the bed, first removed his boots, and then his trousers. When she completely freed his erection from confinement it leaped straight out at her and she gasped in appreciation. Taking it in both her hands she leaned forward and kissed the tip, then ran her tongue over the entire length until he was good and wet. After that she went back to the tip, while pumping it with one hand. She certainly knew exactly what she was doing.

When she finally opened her mouth wide and engulfed him totally, Clint almost lost his mind. The heat of her mouth was intense, and she used her tongue, lips and teeth to bring him waves of pleasure so intense it was almost painful. When he felt his cock straining for release, she suddenly tightened her hand around the base.

"Oh, not yet, my lovely," she said, speaking directly to his penis, "not yet. I'm not finished with you."

She stood up, put her hand against his chest and pushed him down onto his back. Then she crawled up onto him, so that she was sitting on his chest with her pussy pressed against his face.

"But first," she said, "it's my turn for some pleasure . . ."

He was only too happy to oblige. The scent of her wet vagina filled his nose, and he proceeded to lick and suck her so that she was gushing onto his face, also wetting his neck and chest with her nectar.

Finally, he felt her body tremble as she grabbed hold of the bedpost and started bouncing up and down on him, biting her lip to keep from screaming. Just when he thought she might suffocate him, she was gone, once again down between his legs, sucking him.

She continued until he was good and wet, then mounted him. They were both so moist that he slid right into her. She rode him that way for a short time, then hopped off and said, "Move!"

He slid over on the bed, thinking she wanted to lie next to him, but instead she got onto her hands and knees and said, "Like this. Hurry, hurry!"

He got to his knees behind her, slid his cock up between her thighs and into her wet pussy. After he'd poked her that way for just a few seconds, she said, "Okay, you're wet enough!"

He knew what she wanted, and was surprised. He withdrew, and she actually reached behind herself, gripped her ass cheeks and spread them.

"Now!"

His cock, still gleaming with her juices, plunged right into her anus.

"Yes!" she said, removing her hands and grabbing the bedpost. "Oh, yes."

Her demands only excited him more, and he began to slam in and out of her harder and harder. He literally forgot about who she was, how old she was, and where they were. All that mattered was what was happening between them at that moment.

When he exploded into her he bellowed out his pleasure and pain, and then she screamed . . .

"I'm sorry I screamed," she said, later, lying on her back next to him.

"As long as you're all right."

"Oh, I'm fine," she said, "I'm so fine." She reached over and grabbed his cock. "Thank you, thank you."

He began to swell in her hand. Her eyes widened and she stroked him until he was hard again, then mounted him, took her inside and said, "Thank . . . you!"

***

Later still he said, "I have to go."

"Why?" she asked.

"Because if I stay, I won't be able to walk by morning. You'll see to that."

She chuckled and said, "Yes, but that would be true of both of us."

"Besides," he said, "I have things to do."

He got up off the bed and started to get dressed. She propped herself up on her elbow, her body covered by the sheet.

"Not such a mousy little bank clerk, huh?" she asked, smiling.

Chapter Twenty-Nine

There were several smaller saloons in town, but Clint felt sure that the two strangers would either go to the Black Horse or the River Run. Black Horse if they wanted to gamble, River Run if they wanted to see Stacy. He decided to check the River Run, first.

As he entered the busy saloon he saw Angela right away, carrying a tray of drinks from the bar and wearing almost nothing at all. Her dress was cut low to show the tops of her breasts, and slit up high so that the men could see her leg and thigh. He knew it would be no time before she had a volunteer to go upstairs with her and pay for a poke. She saw him and smiled, waved with one hand while balancing the tray with the other.

He claimed a place at the end of the bar furthest from the window. No point in giving a bushwhacker a clear shot. Once he had a beer in hand he just waited, and soon enough Angela came over to him.

"Miss me?" she asked.

"Desperately."

"Not likely." She leaned in and sniffed him. "You already been with somebody."

"You can tell?"

"Oh, yeah," she said. "I just hope it wasn't Stacy."

"It wasn't," he said. "Not tonight, anyway."

"You hear lookin' for somethin', someone, or just drinkin'?" she asked.

"I'm looking for someone."

"Who?"

"Two strangers rode into town this morning," he said. "I don't know what they look like, but—"

"Don't matter," she said. "They're over there, sittin' at a table."

"Where?"

"I ain't gonna point," she scolded him. "There." She jerked her chin. "One black hat, one grey, drinkin' whiskey."

"I see them."

"What do you want with 'em?" she asked.

"Just wondering if they're looking for trouble."

"Well, I'll tell ya one thing," she said, "they ain't lookin' for me."

"Fools," he said.

"Right?"

"Who are they looking for?"

"They were talkin' to Stacy for a little while, but she ain't been back to their table since."

"Did she look happy to see them?"

"Not very," Angela said.

"How long did they talk?"

"A few minutes," she said. "She didn't even sit down with 'em."

"Well," Clint said, "maybe I will."

She leaned against the bar with her elbows resting on it. "What can I do to help?"

"Why do you want to?"

"Because maybe it'll make Stacy mad."

"Good enough," Clint said. "When I walk over there and sit down, you bring three beers."

"Okay!"

Clint walked to the table. The two men were talking intently to each other, as he sat down. They both looked at him in total surprise.

"How are you fellas doing?" he asked.

"Wha—" the handsome man started.

"Who the hell are you?" the homely man asked.

But before he could answer, Angela appeared with three beers on a tray.

"Here you go," she said, setting them down. "Enjoy, fellas."

"We didn't ask for these," the handsome man said.

"That's okay," Clint said. "They're on me. Thanks, Angela."

"Sure." She flounced away.

"Drink up, boys," Clint said, picking up his glass.

Neither man touched theirs.

"What's the idea?" the handsome one asked.

"I just thought we should get acquainted," Clint said.

"Why's that?" the homely man asked.

"Well," Clint said, "you two are here to rob a bank, and I'm here to stop you. So I just thought we should meet."

The two men exchanged a glance, and then the handsome one said, "What the hell are you talkin' about? Who the hell are you?"

"My name's Clint Adams."

The homely man gaped. "The Gunsmith?"

"That's right."

The homely man swallowed audibly, but the handsome man said, "Are we supposed to be impressed? Or scared?"

"Concerned, maybe," Clint said. "Didn't Stacy tell you I was here?"

"Stacy . . . who?" the handsome man asked.

"Oh, come on," Clint said. "Let's not make this harder than it has to be. You were already seen talking to her."

"Is she one of these girls?" the handsome man asked.

"Actually, she's not, is she?" Clint asked. "She's just playing one, like Mark Crawford is pretending to be a bank teller. You see? I know everything."

The two men stared at him.

Clint looked around.

"Maybe we should call Stacy over to join the party."

Chapter Thirty

"Maybe," the handsome man said, "you better get the hell out of here or, Gunsmith or not, we'll throw you out."

"Merritt—"

"Shut up!" the handsome man said.

Merritt. Clint had one name.

"That's okay, friend," he said to the homely man. "I just wanted to make contact, let you know I was here. Maybe you can now talk Stacy and Crawford out of robbing the Truxton Bank." He stood up. "Enjoy the beers."

He turned and walked right out through the batwing doors.

***

As Clint left, Felton quickly picked up the beer and drank half of it.

"What are you doin'?" Merritt demanded.

"My mouth's dry!" Felton said. "That was the goddamned Gunsmith."

"I know who it was."

"And he knows why we're here," Felton said.

"He's guessin'."

"Well, he's guessin' pretty damn good," Felton said. "We gotta get out of town."

"Relax—"

"How can you tell me to relax?"

"—relax, damn it!" Merritt hissed. "We just have to find out from Stacy what's goin' on."

Felton picked up the beer mug and drained it, then poured himself a shot of whiskey.

"Take deep breaths," Merritt told him. "We can't panic."

"Easy for you to say."

"Not so easy," Merritt said, "but I'm sayin' it anyway. Just relax." He looked around. "We have to get Stacy over here."

But when he finally spotted her, he didn't have to wave her down. She was already coming toward them.

***

Stacy did not see Clint Adams enter the saloon, but she did see him sitting with Merritt and Felton. She watched as Angela brought over their beers, and then the three men spoke. Finally, Adams stood up and left. She saw that Felton, the homely man, was in a panic, but she knew Merritt would keep him from bolting. She also knew she had to get over there before the panic spread from one man to the other.

She started for their table, trying not to run.

***

"What the fuck—" Felton started when she reached their table, but Merritt put his hand on the man's arm to silence him.

Stacy sat in the chair vacated by the Gunsmith just moments before.

"That was the Gunsmith!" Felton hissed.

"I know who it was," she said. "What did he want?"

"He wanted us to know that he knows we're here to rob the bank," Merritt said. "How does she know that, Stacy?"

"He doesn't <u>know</u>," she said, "he's guessin'."

"And why is he guessin'?"

"He recognized Mark when he went into the bank."

"From where?" Merritt demanded.

"Some town in Missouri from ten years ago, when Mark robbed it with some friends of his."

"Jesus," Felton said.

"Take it easy," she said. "All that means is that he knows Mark robbed a bank ten years ago."

"And now he works in one," Merritt said. "What a coincidence."

"Exactly," Stacy said. "A coincidence."

Merritt leaned forward.

"You want us to go ahead with this job," he said to her, "you better do somethin' about this."

"I intend to," she promised. "Just stay calm. I'll get back to you."

She stood up and walked away.

"Stay calm," Felton said. "Easy for her to say."

"Maybe not," Merritt said. "She's been here longer than we have."

Felton poured himself another shot of whiskey.

"Take it easy on that stuff," Merritt told him. "We gotta stay calm."

"Look," Felton said, "I ain't no fast gun. I ain't lookin' forward to facin' the Gunsmith. Maybe you are."

"No, you know I ain't a fast gun, neither," Merritt said.

"Then let's get the hell out of here," Felton said. "There are other banks."

There may have been other banks, but for Merritt, there was no other woman.

"Let's give Stacy a chance to deal with this," he said. "All we have to do is stay in town and out of trouble. You got it?"

"Yeah, yeah, I got it."

"Or maybe you wanna leave," Merritt went on. "That's up to you."

"No, no," Felton said, "I'm with you, Jeff. We'll give Stacy a chance."

Chapter Thirty-One

Stacy wasn't sure what to do, so she went to her room to figure it out. But she was still in the middle of her shift. If she went to her room now, she'd get fired.

Unless she took a man with her.

She didn't want to take Merritt or Felton. It wouldn't do any good for them to know she was trying to figure things out. She wanted them to think—to know—that she already had it figured.

So she needed a man she could take upstairs, but not have to do anything with so she could think. Somebody so drunk they wouldn't notice.

After walking around the saloon for ten minutes, she found him. He was seated at a table alone, his head bent over a mug of beer. To the naked eye, he was asleep.

She walked over and sat across from him.

"Hi."

He jerked his head up, opened his eyes and looked at her.

"Oh, hi." He was in his later forties, faded looking, worn, tired and sad.

"Want a poke?" she asked.

"Huh?" He was bleary-eyed, couldn't seem to focus. But he was a better choice than she had originally thought.

"A poke," she said. "Wanna go upstairs?"

"I—I don't got the money."

"That's okay," she said. "It's free."

He frowned. "Free?"

"Sure," she said, "my gift to you." She stood up, put out her hand. "Come on."

Hesitantly, he took it and she helped him out of his chair. He was a few inches shorter than she was. People watched them curiously as she led him to the stairs, and up.

She took him down the hall, into her room, and locked the door, then pushed him down on the bed. As he watched she stripped naked, and his eyes grew wider as her nipples and snatch came into view.

"J-Jesus . . ." he breathed. "I ain't n-never seen nothin' so beautiful before."

"What's your name?"

"Dean."

"Thank you, Dean."

She knelt down in front of him and removed his boots, then pulled off his trousers. When his cock came into view it was impressive, even soft. She reached out and touched it, and he jumped, but it began to swell.

She decided to go ahead and fuck him.

Her first intention was to get him to fall asleep, then do her thinking before waking him up and telling him he was great. Now she thought. She could think while riding him.

"You just lie on your back," she said.

"My shirt—"

"You can leave your shirt on," she said, squeezing his penis. "This is the important part, right?"

"Uh, yeah . . ." He closed his eyes as she stroked him to fullness.

"Come on," she said, putting her other hand against his chest, "lay back."

He got on his back on her bed. She mounted him, her pussy already wet, took him inside and sat down on him hard.

"Oh, Jesus—" he gasped.

She started to ride him up and down, closing her eyes. She felt excited, but she also felt calm. He filled her up. She only hoped he would last long enough for her to come up with a solution.

She rode him up and down and let her mind drift . . .

***

Clint Adams went back to his hotel room, barricaded his door with the wooden chair beneath the door knob, and once again set the pitcher-and-basin on the windowsill. When that was all done he removed his gunbelt and boots and sat on the bed to relax.

He was going to have to give the two men time to complain to Stacy about him, and decide if they were still going to stick to the plan—whatever the plan was. Then Stacy would have to talk to Crawford. It would suit Clint for all of them to just leave town and go looking for another bank to rob.

But somehow, having spent time with Stacy, he didn't think that was likely.

***

Dean was asleep.

He hadn't lasted as long as she had hoped, and when she felt he was about to blow, she hopped off and let him shoot gobs of cum all over himself and the bed. Then he fell asleep, drunk and exhausted . . .

She sat on the edge of the bed, still naked, her hand between her legs while she finished her figuring.

She knew somebody had taken a shot at Clint Adams. She didn't know who. But it wasn't her, and she doubted it was Mark Crawford. Merritt and Felton weren't in town at that time. If whoever it was hadn't missed, the whole mess would be solved.

But if it happened again, successfully, it would take Adams out of the equation. And whoever took that first shot would get the blame.

She closed her eyes as her legs began to tremble and her orgasm approached. Lying back in a prone position, she continued to drive her own fingers in and out of herself, all the while contemplating her plan . . .

***

She needed Mark Crawford to do something for her, which might put Clint Adams at ease, to some extent. Adams just needed to be relaxed a little, and then somebody could be able to kill him.

She could get Merritt to do it. All she had to do was go with him to his room the next day, and fuck him until, he agreed. It was the way she always got her way with him. She preferred not to use that technique with Felton, or with Mark

Crawford. She had other ways to manipulate Mark, and Merritt could handle Felton.

So she just needed to fuck Jeff Merritt into killing the Gunsmith.

Chapter Thirty-Two

Well before morning Stacy woke Dean, told him he was wonderful, cleaned him up as much as she could, and pushed him out the door.

"Can't we go again?" he asked, hopefully.

"Sorry," she said. "I give out one free poke a month, and that was it."

"How about next month?"

"We'll see."

After he was gone she changed the sheets on her bed, wadded up the soiled ones and tossed them in a corner to be thrown away. Then she went back to work.

In the morning she was determined to get to Mark Crawford before he got to the bank. She was waiting for him across the street when he came out of his rooming house.

"Are you crazy?" he asked. "If Emma sees you she'll kick me out."

"Don't worry about that," she said. "Once we take the bank you can buy this house and kick her out."

"So we're goin' ahead with the plan?"

"Yes," she said, "Merritt and Felton are here. We'll move forward with the plan, but first you're going to confess to Clint Adams that you are—or were—a bank robber."

"What?"

"I'll explain," she said. "Walk with me . . ."

When Mark Crawford got to work at the Truxton Bank he immediately went to the manager's office and knocked on the door.

"Come!"

He entered, closed the door firmly behind him as Nathan Winslow looked up at him.

"What is it, Mark?"

"I need some time off this morning, Mr. Winslow," he said.

"Oh? Is there a problem?"

"Nothin' I can't handle," Crawford said. "It'll take me about an hour."

"Does this have to do with—you know, our plan?"

"It does, yes."

"Well, all right," Winslow said. "An hour. No more."

"Yes, sir."

Crawford left the office and headed for the front door.

"Trouble this morning, Mark?" Tilly asked.

He stopped, looked at the older woman, her wire-framed glasses and grey-streaked hair in a bun. She was a nice lady.

"Nothin' major, Tilly," he said. "I should be back in an hour. I cleared it with Mr. Winslow."

"Well," she said, "be careful out there."

"I will, Tilly."

He left the bank.

Clint came out of his hotel and was surprised to see Mark Crawford hurrying toward him. He should have been in the bank, which would just be opening.

"Adams," he said, "we need to talk."

"Well," Clint said, "I'm going to breakfast. If you want, you can tag along."

"I already ate breakfast at Emma's—"

"Then you can have a cup of coffee while we talk."

This clearly was not what the younger man had expected, but he relented and said, "Yeah, okay."

Clint led the way to Cody Smithers' café.

"Here?" Crawford asked. "I never ate here before."

"I have. The food's very good," Clint said. "Not as good as Emma Cleary's, but close."

They entered, found the place empty except for one table that was occupied by a man and a woman and a little girl.

"'mornin', Mr. Adams," Smithers said, "Any table."

Clint took one in the back, sat with Mark Crawford, who looked around uncomfortably.

"Relax," Clint said. "Somebody took a shot at me in the dark, but I don't think they'll try anything this morning. That is, unless it was you?"

"What?" Crawford asked. "Me? Why should I take a shot at you?"

"You tell me," Clint said.

Smithers knew what Clint wanted for breakfast, and brought over a plate of steak-and-eggs. He poured coffee for both men, and moved away.

"What do you want to tell me?" Clint asked.

"It's about Missouri," Crawford said.

"Ten Pines?"

Crawford nodded.

"Look," he said, "I did rob a bank back then. You're right about me. I was a bank robber."

"Was?"

"That's right," Crawford said. "I went straight after that. Well, not right after that, but after a few more jobs went bad."

"And Stacy? What about her?"

"She was involved with some of the jobs I was on," he said, "but she's gone straight, too. Look, Adams, we're both tryin' to make lives for ourselves."

"Not together?" Clint asked. "You're not a couple?"

"No," the bank teller said. "We're friends, that's all."

"And the others?"

"What others?"

"Well, gangs aren't usually made up of one man and one woman," Clint pointed out.

"Well, sure, there were others, but they're not here."

"Where are they?"

"I don't know," Crawford said. "We all went our own ways."

"So the two strangers who rode into town yesterday aren't with you and Stacy?"

"What two strangers?" Crawford said.

"They were talking to Stacy in the saloon."

"That's her job," he said. "Talkin' to men, takin' them upstairs."

"And that's better than robbing banks?"

"You'd have to ask her." Crawford left the coffee untouched and stood up. "I have to go to work. I've told you the truth, Mr. Adams. I hope you won't ruin what I've built here for myself."

"I wouldn't want to ruin anything for you, Mark . . ."

"Thank you."

"If you're telling the truth," Clint finished.

"How can I prove it to you?"

"I don't know," Clint said. "I guess only time will tell."

Crawford looked as if he was going to say something else, but then just shrugged helplessly and left.

Chapter Thirty-Three

Clint finished his meal, wondering what the point of confessing at this point was. He was already sure of his identifications—Crawford was the man he recognized from the Missouri bank, Stacy was working with him, and now those two strangers had ridden into town.

Stacy was a smart girl. If it was anybody's idea for Mark to confess, it was hers. What was the point, though? To throw him off? To make him careless, as if knowing the truth would somehow accomplish that?

So something was up, but what? And he still didn't know who had taken a shot at him. Crawford didn't seem likely, and neither did Stacy. It might have been someone with no connection to either one of them, just a random person who recognized him and decided to make a try. It had happened many times before, and he had not always found out who the shooter was. Very often when they missed they lit out, never to be heard from again, having missed their one shot at becoming famous.

He finished his breakfast and paid Smithers for the meal.

"You know," Smithers said, "I may have to make you a partner. You're pretty much supportin' me, anyway."

"Don't worry," Clint said, "I'm recommending you to everyone."

"I appreciate that."

The Bank Job

Clint left the café, decided to go see Sheriff Irving and find out if he knew anything about the two strangers.

***

Irving was standing in front of his gun rack when Clint entered, apparently examining his rifles and shotguns.

"Adams," he said, turning. "What can I do for you?"

"A couple of strangers rode into town yesterday," Clint said. "I was wondering if you knew anything about them?"

"Just that they rode in, got a room in one of the smaller, cheaper hotels, and they've done some drinkin' at both the Black Horse and River Run."

Clint studied the man for a moment. Maybe he was better at his job than he had first thought.

"How about you?" Irving asked. "Any more information about bank robbers?"

Clint looked over at the coffee pot. The strong smell of it was filling the office.

"Coffee?" Irving asked.

"Don't mind if I do."

The lawman poured two mugs, gave one to Clint, then sat at his desk.

"Have a seat."

Clint sat across from him.

"What've you got?"

"I had a visit from the teller today, Mark Crawford."

"What'd he wanna do, confess?" Irving asked, jokingly.

"Yes."

The sheriff almost choked.

"What?"

"He told me that he did rob a bank in Ten Pines, Missouri ten years ago, and a few after that, but now he's going straight."

"Jesus," Irving said. "Did you believe him?"

"The first part, yeah," Clint said. "I knew he robbed the Missouri bank, but I doubt that he's going straight."

"Anything else?"

"He told me Stacy's going straight, as well," Clint said. "And when I asked him about the two strangers. He claimed not to know what I was talking about."

"So why'd he confess?"

"That's what I'm wondering," Clint said. "I think they're trying to throw me off balance."

"And have they?"

"Not at all."

"What about the shot?" Irving asked. "You think they had anythin' to do with it?"

"No, not them," Clint said. "Whether or not they had somebody else do it, I can't say."

"Those two strangers?"

"Could be," Clint said. "Maybe they got here earlier, took the shot, then rode out and made it look like they just rode in yesterday."

"Why do I hear an 'or?'"

"Or," Clint said, "somebody else took the shot, missed, and lit out."

"And it has nothin' to do with the bank," Irving said, "and everything to do with you bein' the Gunsmith."

"Right."

"So what's your plan now?"

"If they're trying to throw me off balance," Clint said, "then they'll make a move. I'll just have to wait. Somehow, I don't think they'll go ahead with their bank job while I'm still around."

"What if they just give it up and move on?"

"That'd suit you, I know," Clint said, "but I don't think that's going to be the case."

"So it's a waitin' game?"

"It's always been that," Clint said, "unless I can come up with something that'll force them to make a move sooner."

"You got anybody to watch your back now that there might be four of 'em?"

"Just you, Sheriff," Clint said. "Just you."

Chapter Thirty-Four

Stacy knocked on the door and when Jeff Merritt opened it she smiled and looked past him.

"Is Felton here?"

"He's got his own room," Merritt said.

"Well, that's good news. You gonna invite me in?"

"That depends," Merritt said. "You in a friendly mood today?"

She reached up to touch the string that held her dress cinched at the top, then yanked on it.

"Do you want me to show you how friendly," she asked, "out here in the hall?"

Merritt growled, "Get in here!" reached out, and dragged her into the room.

He pulled her dress off and tossed her, naked, onto the bed. Stacy knew what Merritt liked. He enjoyed being in control and on top, but he never lasted very long.

She watched as he undressed. He was a good-looking man, with a very nice looking penis. It was too bad he didn't know how to use it.

When he was naked he climbed on top of her and hurriedly stuffed himself into her. She wrapped her arms and legs around him, cooed into his ear, urged him on, and milked him dry with her insides.

When he was done he rolled over, crossed his arms over his eyes.

"Who-eee," he said. "I missed that!"

"It has been a while," she said.

"Yeah?" he said. "And who's fault is that?"

"Nobody's," she said. "It was just part of the plan. And speakin' of the plan . . ."

"Yeah?"

"The Gunsmith has to go, Jeff," she said. "He's in the way."

"Yeah? Tell me somethin' I don't know."

"I'm telln' you that you hafta kill him," she said. "You and Felton."

"Felton ain't about to face the Gunsmith."

"Nobody said anythin' about facin' him," she said.

"You mean bushwhack 'im? Back shoot 'im?"

"We hafta get him out of the way," she said. "What does it matter how we do it?"

"It don't," Merritt said.

"We need to do it soon."

"Just gimme a minute and we'll go again." She knew he was talking about the sex.

"Yeah, sure," she said.

In moments he was fast asleep.

She got up, dressed and left.

Chapter Thirty-Five

Clint decided to give Mark Crawford another push by going to see the bank manager, Nathan Winslow. He didn't expect to get much from the man, he just wanted the teller to see him going into the manager's office, to give him something to think about.

As he entered the bank, though, Crawford wasn't the only teller to spot him. Tilly also saw him and smiled, although she made no gesture. It was a secret smile, just between them.

He didn't bother speaking to any one, just walked to the bank manager's door and knocked.

"Come!"

Winslow looked up from his desk as Clint entered the office.

"Mr. Adams," he said, surprised. "It's common for visitors to be announced first."

"They seemed busy out there," Clint said, "so I came straight back. Is that a problem?"

"Well, no, not really," Winslow said. "Have a seat. What's this about? Have you decided to open an account with that money Mr. Jameson paid you?"

"No," Clint said, "that's not it."

"Then what is it?"

"It's your teller, Mark Crawford."

"Oh, that again?" Winslow said. "Do you still think he's a bank robber?"

"I know he is," Clint said. "So do you."

"That's preposterous!"

"I never told you I recognized him as a bank robber," Clint said. "That means he must have told you."

Winslow immediately realized his mistake, but just as quickly tried to recover.

"Yes, he told me when he applied here that he had once robbed a bank."

"Once," Clint said. "And you hired him, anyway?"

"I believe in second chances," the man said. "Besides, he was honest with me."

"I see."

"You don't believe in second chances?"

"I don't believe men change," Clint said. "Not deep down."

"That's a shame."

"I've seen too many examples of it," Clint said.

"Well," Winslow said, "that's neither here nor there. I hired him, and I like his work ethic."

"I think he's planning to rob you."

"Nonsense."

"Him, a woman named Stacy, and two strangers in town. I think they have a plan."

"Why haven't they done it, then?"

"Because I'm here."

"Isn't that a little . . . conceited?"

"Possibly," Clint said. "Still, that's what I believe. They won't try it while I'm in town."

"So do you intend to remain in town forever?"

"Not at all," Clint said. "I've spoken to the sheriff, told him what I believe."

Winslow shook his head. "I'm afraid our sheriff is not the most dedicated lawman I've ever met."

"Be that as it may," Clint said, "if they try while I'm here, I'll stop them. And if you're involved—"

"Now see here—" Winslow started.

"That's the only reason I can see for you hiring a bank robber to be a teller in your bank," Clint said, cutting him off. "You intend to rob the bank, yourself."

"I have been the manager of this bank for over ten years!" Winslow blustered. "Why on earth would I want to rob it?"

"Maybe," Clint said, "because you've been the manager for ten years."

***

As he left the bank he again got a stare from Crawford, and a secret smile from Tilly.

Once outside he leaned against a post and thought about his brief meeting with the bank manager. How happy can a man be to have the same job for ten years? Clint knew that he would hate it, and he knew a lot of men who would, also. Most men holding jobs like that were looking to move up. Perhaps it was Winslow's inability to do so that would lead to his involvement in a bank robbery.

He stepped down into the street, waited for a couple of wagons to go by, then crossed over to the other side. That put him right in front of the Black Horse Saloon, so he decided to go inside for a beer.

It wasn't in full swing; getting a place at the bar was easy. He leaned his elbows on it and gave the bartender a nod.

"Beer," he called out.

"Comin' up!"

The bartender brought it over and set it down in front of him.

"No hard feelin's, huh?" he said.

"What?"

"It was me who told the sheriff you was watchin' the bank," the man said. "No hard feelin's, I hope."

"Naw, that's okay," Clint said. "What's your name?"

"Leo."

"Well, Leo, a free beer would go a long way towards making sure there aren't any hard feelings."

"Done!" the man said. "But hey, if you don't mind me askin' . . ."

"Go ahead."

"Yer still lookin' at the bank now, Mr. Adams," Leo said. "How come?"

"Well, Leo," Clint said, "I'm fairly certain there's going to be a robbery attempt."

"Oh yeah? Who by? Is there some gang ridin' into town to rob it?"

"No," Clint said, "the people planning the job are already here."

"Geez," Leo said. "You tell the sheriff?"

"I sure did."

139

"Well, I guess that's all ya can do, right?" Leo asked. "Tell the law, and watch the bank."

"Right."

Now the barman joined Clint with his elbows on the bar.

"But you ain't gonna tell me who's involved. Huh?"

"Leo," Clint said, thinking about the bank manager, "you'd never believe me."

Chapter Thirty-Six

Clint was nursing his second beer when the Black Horse started to get busy. Storekeepers had locked up and come in for a drink before they headed home, and ranch hands had finished their work days and ridden to town for some fun. Clint looked around, wondered how many of these hands were from his friend, Dave Jameson's, ranch.

He found out without asking.

"Hey, Mister Adams!" a young hand called out.

Clint didn't recognize him from Jameson's ranch, but then he had done his work, tracking the rustlers, alone.

"Hey," the young man said to his friends, "this is the boss's friend who got back our cattle. Can we buy you another beer, sir?"

"Sure," Clint said, "why not?"

"You're the Gunsmith, ain'tcha?" one of the others asked.

"That's right," Clint said, accepting his fresh drink from the bartender.

"Wow, the boss sure is lucky to have you for a friend," the second man said. "You took care of them rustlers all on your own."

"Well," Clint said, "they were rustlers, not gunmen."

"Still," a third hand said, "there was six of 'em, wasn't there?"

"I heard there were ten!" the first man said.

Clint looked at the young hands, all arguing over how many rustlers there were. He wondered if he should bother telling them there were only three.

He decided to just keep quiet and drink his beer.

***

Stacy saw Mark Crawford come rushing into the River Run and look around at the growing crowd. She knew he was trying to find her.

Stacy grabbed Angela and said, "See that fella there?"

"The bank teller who looks like he's in a panic?" the blonde asked.

"Yeah," Stacy said, "get him to sit at a table, will ya? And bring him a beer?"

"Sure thing," Angela said. "You want me to sit with him, too? Maybe take him upstairs?"

"No," Stacy said, "just get him to stay. If he asks for me, tell him I'll be along shortly."

"Why not?" Angela said. "I got some of my own regulars comin' in, but I'll sit 'im down for ya."

"Thanks."

Angela worked her way through the burgeoning crowd of drinkers, linked her arm through Mark Crawford's and said something into his ear. He nodded and let her lead him to a table.

Stacy continued to watch Crawford fidget while Angela went to get him a beer. She was waiting for Merritt and Felton to come in, and didn't need Crawford to be there with his nerves on display.

She hadn't seen Merritt since being with him in his room. When he arrived she had to make sure he knew what he was supposed to do. He and Felton had to kill the Gunsmith, so they could get on with their business.

Angela brought Crawford his beer, put her hand on his shoulder, said something to him, and then left. The bank teller/bank robber sipped his beer and continued to look around nervously.

She had no choice. She had to go over and sit with Crawford, and get him calmed down. Then she would get him the hell out of the saloon before the other two arrived, so he didn't infect them with his nerves.

Chapter Thirty-Seven

Clint had enough of the rambling and babbling of the young ranch hands, so he thanked them for the drink, bought them all a round, and left.

Outside it was still daylight, with dusk about an hour away. He easily recognized the two men walking across the street as the strangers he'd spoken to in the River Run.

As he watched them he became convinced they were on their way to the saloon, probably to see Stacy. He decided to follow them, but stay on his side of the street.

They led him right to the River Run.

***

"You have to go," Stacy said.

"But why was Adams there?" Crawford demanded.

"Didn't you ask Winslow?"

"No," he said. "I think he'd lie to me."

"Why?"

"I don't trust him."

Again, she asked, "Why?"

"He's a rich man," Crawford said. "Why is he gettin' involved with us?"

"Maybe he's not as rich as you think."

"He's gotta be. He's the bank manager."

"There's money in the bank," Stacy said. "That doesn't mean it's in his pocket."

"They must've been talkin' about me."

"Then maybe you should ask Winslow," Stacy said, "but I need you to get out of here."

"Why?"

"I don't want people seein' you look so nervous," she said. "And I don't want Merritt and Felton to see it."

"Are they here?" He looked around.

"No, but they will be," Stacy said. "We're gonna make plans to get rid of Adams."

"How?"

"Never mind," Stacy said, growing annoyed. "Mark, you have to get out of here, get ahold of yourself, and calm down, then tomorrow go and talk to Winslow."

"Yeah, okay."

She stood up. "Come on. Go now."

He nodded, turned and walked to the batwing doors. As he went out and turned right, Merritt and Felton were coming from the left.

"There's the kid," Felton said.

"Not such a kid," Merritt said. "He just looks young."

"Should I get 'im?"

"No, let 'im go," Merritt said. "I wanna talk to Stacy without him around."

The two men entered the saloon.

Across the street Clint saw Merritt and Felton avoid Mark Crawford. With the woman, Stacy, calling the shots, he was sure each man thought he was getting something different.

He crossed the street and peered in the front window of the River Run. There was a crowd, but he knew who he was looking for, so he easily spotted the two men and, across the room, Stacy.

He wondered if he ought to go after the bank robber-turned-bank teller and play with his head a bit more, but he decided to go into the River Run, instead. That would give Stacy and her two friends something to think about. Or maybe they'd go ahead and make a move in the saloon.

He went through the batwing doors and headed straight to the bar.

***

As soon as Clint had a beer in his hand, the cute blonde Angela was right by his side.

"Bet I know who you're lookin' for," she said, standing next to him, emulating his position with his back to the bar, elbows resting on it.

"Oh? Who might that be?"

"Stacy."

"Why would I be looking for her when I've got you here?" he asked.

"Oh, don't play with a girl, Mr. Adams," she said. "If I thought you were here for me I'd drag you upstairs right now and give you one on the house."

"Now that," Clint said, "sounds like something I might come in here looking for."

She took her elbows off the bar and turned to face him. Beyond her he saw Stacy watching them. Why not go upstairs with this cute blonde? It might just nudge Stacy and her men into a move.

"Are you foolin' me?"

"Not at all."

"Well, all right then!" she said, grabbing his hand and dragging him to the stairs.

Chapter Thirty-Eight

"Where is he?" Merritt asked.

Stacy had just come over and joined them at their table.

"He went upstairs with Angela," she said. "I don't understand it."

"Are you jealous?" Felton asked, smiling.

"No, you idiot," she said. "He's interested in us, so why's he goin' upstairs with her?"

"She's cute," Felton said. "Why not?"

"He's makin' himself an easy target," she explained. "Her room is a shoe box. If you kicked open the door and started shooting, there's no way you could miss."

"Then maybe that's what we should do," Merritt said.

"No," she said, shaking her head, "that won't do."

"Why not? You said you didn't care how we did it," Merritt reminded her.

"Use your head," Stacy said. "He's invitin' us there,"

"You mean he's sittin' on the other side of the door, waitin' with his gun out?" Felton asked.

"Somethin' like that, yeah," she said.

"What a waste," Felton said, shaking his head. "That blonde's really cute."

"Really?" Stacy asked. "That's what you're thinkin' right now?"

"Okay, never mind," Merritt said, getting between Stacy and Felton. "When do you suggest we kill 'im?"

"I told you, I don't care where or how you do it," she said. "I just don't think you should do it when he expects it."

"He's the Gunsmith, Stacy," Merritt said, "He always expects somebody to kill 'im."

Stacy looked over at the stairs. She wondered if Adams was really waiting for them, or if he was involved with Angela.

"Wait here," she said, starting to rise.

Merritt grabbed her wrist.

"Where are you goin'?"

"I just wanna have a listen at Angela's door," she said. "If they really are in her bed then maybe this is the time to go after him."

Merritt released her wrist and watched her walk to the stairs.

***

Stacy went up the stairs casually, but when she reached the second floor she was out of sight of anyone on the saloon floor. She crept down the hall, past her own room, to Angela's door, avoiding places on the floor she knew had noisy boards. Pressing her ear to the door she listened intently. She thought she heard voices, then Angela's noisy bedsprings. Once the springs began singing their tune, she hurried back downstairs.

***

"So whataya think?" Felton asked.

"I think you better check your gun, make sure it's loaded," Merritt said, doing just that.

"So we're gonna go upstairs and shoot him while he's in bed with the cute blonde?"

"That depends on what Stacy has to say when she comes back down."

"Well," Felton said, looking over at the stairs, "we ain't got long to wait."

Merritt glanced that way and saw Stacy rushing across the floor to them, ducking around customers, doing everything she could not to run.

"Do it!" she said, sitting down.

"Are they going at it?" Merritt said.

"Angela's got a tiny room and noisy bedsprings," Stacy said. "We always know when she has a man in there. Right now, those things are makin' a racket!" She seemed very excited.

"Okay," Merritt said. "Only once we do it, we can't come runnin' back through here."

"There's a stairway in the back, leads to a door in the rear that will take you to the alley. From there you can get any-where."

"And where should we get to?" Felton asked.

"Just go back to your hotel and wait," Stacy said. "Once Adams is taken care of, we'll be ready to do the job."

"And I'll be seein' you before that?" Merritt asked.

"Oh, you'll be seein' me," she said.

Merritt and Felton stood up and walked slowly across the room. When they got to the stairs they tried to go up nice and casual.

Stacy just sat and waited for the shots.

***

Merritt and Felton started down the hall and drew their guns. Stacy had told them what room to go to, and what floorboards to watch out for. When they reached it they looked at each other, and Merritt nodded. Felton lifted his foot, kicked in the door, and they darted into the room, guns ready.

Just at that moment Merritt realized they hadn't heard any bedsprings.

A door opened across the hall and Clint Adams stepped out.

"What took you so long?" he asked.

Chapter Thirty-Nine

Stacy knew two things immediately. There were too few shots, and they were from too few guns.

Moments after the shooting stopped, Angela came running to the top of the stairs.

"Somebody get the sheriff!"

Nobody moved at first, because the blonde was half-naked. But finally several men reacted and ran out the batwing doors.

Stacy remained seated where she was, feigning disinterest in the proceedings, but inside she was desperate to know who was dead. She didn't care who was alive. It would have suited her just as well if all three men were dead, just as long as the Gunsmith was out of the way.

She forced herself to sit there, and wait.

***

"Now just take it easy—" Clint had started to say to the two men, but they were shocked into action, and couldn't help themselves. They already had their guns out, and both turned to train them on Clint. He reacted the only way he knew how in a situation like that. It involved self-preservation, clear and simple.

He drew and fired.

Clint Adams never drew his gun unless he was going to use it, and when he fired he rarely—if ever—missed. In the confined space of that hallway, there was even less chance of that happening.

Each man took a bullet to the heart, and slumped to the floor without firing a shot.

When Angela came back up the hall Clint said, "You better get yourself dressed."

"You owe me for this," she said. "It was no fun bouncing up and down on that mattress alone."

"Don't worry," he said, "when you and me start bouncing around on a mattress, it won't be that one."

"I'm gonna hold you to that," she said, entering her room and pulling on her dress. "How did you know these two men would be comin' for ya?"

"It was just a possibility," he told her, while reloading his gun, "but a good one."

"I'll say," she agreed.

They both turned when somebody came running up the hall. Clint had holstered his gun, but kept his hand near it until he saw that it was the sheriff.

"What the hell—"

"Angela can tell you, Sheriff," Clint said. "We came up to her room and these two interrupted us."

"That's right, Sheriff," Angela said, having returned from downstairs. "They kept me from makin' my money. If they got any money in their pockets—"

"Never mind, Angela," Sheriff Irving said. "You can go downstairs."

"I'll see you later, Clint," she said, and flounced off down the hall.

"She doesn't seem too upset," Clint commented.

"She works in a saloon," Irving said. "She's seen a lot at a young age. So, tell me about these two. They the ones you thought were here to rob the bank?"

"Two of 'em, yeah."

"Then I guess kilin' them is gonna put a crimp in somebody's plans."

"Unless they were hoping that once I killed them you'd post me out of town. Or they hoped these two would kill me. Either way, they'd be clear to rob the bank."

"Thanks for the confidence," Sheriff Irving said.

"Sorry."

"All right," the lawman said, "the girl backs your story. You can go. I'll get some volunteers to carry these bodies out."

They walked back to the stairs together.

***

Stacy watched as Clint Adams came down the stairs with the sheriff. He still had his gun, though, so he wasn't under arrest. She knew, for sure, that Merritt and Felton were dead.

She wasn't upset that they were dead, she was only upset that he was alive.

***

"I need volunteers," Sheriff Irving said, and then he pointed, "You, you, you and you. Upstairs and move those bodies."

"Bodies?" the bartender, said.

"Yeah, what did you think that shootin' was about?" Irving asked. He looked at his four volunteers. "Go!"

The four men put down their drinks and ran up the stairs.

Irving turned to Clint.

"You go to your hotel and stay there, and don't kill anybody along the way."

"I'll do my best, Sheriff."

As Clint left the saloon Stacy stood and walked up beside Sheriff Irving.

"He killed two men and you're just gonna let him go?" she asked, keeping her tone low.

"They came after him," Irving said. "They got what they deserved. Why, were they friends of yours?"

"Just customers," she said. "I don't like seein' customers get killed. It's bad for business."

Chapter Forty

Clint not only managed to avoid shooting anybody on his way to his hotel, but he also avoided being shot at.

Sitting on his bed with his boots off and his gunbelt on the bedpost, he wondered if this evening's developments were going to change anything. Stacy had looked cold and calm when he came down the stairs with the sheriff, but that didn't mean she wasn't churning inside. He was sure she had sent the two men upstairs to kill him. Now that they were gone, did she have others who were supposed to help her and Mark Crawford rob the bank?

Well, he'd been hoping something would happen, and now it had. The next day was going to be very interesting.

***

Clint came down early in the morning and from the look the desk clerk gave him, he knew news had spread that he killed two men the night before.

He left the hotel, and walked to Smithers' café to have breakfast. The place was empty but he took the same table he had been taking in the past.

"Excitin' time for you last night, from what I hear," Smithers said.

"It was busy," Clint said. "I don't usually find killing men exciting."

"Sorry," Smithers said. "What'll you have this morning?"

"Ham and eggs," Clint said.

"I'll bring the coffee right away."

"Thanks."

Clint had expected a visit from the sheriff early in the morning. He felt certain the lawman was going to ask him to leave town. But even though two of the would-be bank robbers had been dealt with, that still left the lawman with Mark Crawford, Stacy and anyone else they may have drafted to help them. And that wasn't even taking the bank manager, Winslow, into consideration. Clint doubted that Sheriff Irving was keen to deal with a bank robbery. Better to leave that to the Gunsmith, who couldn't mind his own business.

Smithers brought the coffee and said, "Breakfast in two minutes."

"Sure, thanks."

"Did what happened last night provide any answers for you?" the man asked.

"It told me that, so far, I'm thinking right," Clint said. "But that Stacy, she's the brains behind this whole thing, I'm sure of it. I doubt she'd send her only two gunnies after me."

"So there are more?" Smithers asked.

"I'm betting yes, there are more," Clint said. "I just don't know if they're already here, or on the way."

"I hope it works out for you," Smithers said.

It didn't have to work out for Clint, it had to work out for the townspeople who had money in the Truxton Bank, and Smithers was not one of those.

The ham and eggs came and he dug in, washing it down with several cups of coffee.

***

"You're not supposed to come here!" Nathan Winslow hissed as Sheriff Irving entered his office.

"Stop worryin'," Irving said. "Just say I was here to tell you that Clint Adams killed two men he thought were plannin' to rob the bank. That is, if anyone asks."

"What do you want, anyway?" the bank manager asked.

"I'm startin' to have second thoughts."

"About what?"

"About what?" Irving repeated. "About robbin' your bank!"

"Shhhh," Winslow said, "keep your voice down."

"Look," Irving said, "after that saloon girl and your teller came to you with their plan, you came to me. You told me this was gonna be easy."

"It will be easy," Winslow said. "All you have to do is not panic."

"Not panic?" Irving said. "Adams killed two men yesterday—two men who were supposed to help us rob the bank."

"Don't worry, Sheriff," Winslow said. "There are more."

"More men? Where?"

"Look, Stacy and I have this all planned out," Winslow assured him.

"The banker and the saloon girl," Irving said, shaking his head. "What a pair! What the hell was I thinkin'?"

The Bank Job

"You were thinking the same thing I was thinking, Sheriff," Winslow said. "That you've been stuck in this job for too damn long, and it's about time you got what you deserve."

"Yeah, that's what I was thinkin', all right," Sheriff Irving agreed. "And now I'm afraid I am gonna get what's comin' to me."

"Just hang on a little bit longer, Sheriff," Winslow said. "It's all going to turn out just the way we want it to."

"Yeah," Irving said, moving toward the door, "yeah, okay. A little longer."

***

Clint had come out of the café, walked a few blocks and suddenly saw Sheriff Irving coming out of the bank.

What the hell?

Chapter Forty-One

There were a lot of reasons Sheriff Irving could have been in the bank. It couldn't have to have anything to do with the robbery Clint was sure was coming. But if it did, was Sheriff Irving involved? After all, if Clint was going to suspect Nathan Winslow of robbing the bank he had been managing for more than 10 years, then why not suspect the sheriff, who had been in his job almost that long?

Clint might have had second thoughts about what he was doing. If the sheriff and bank manager were involved in a plan to rob the bank, maybe the town should just handle this whole thing, itself. But since he now had two killings on his hands, he couldn't just ride out and forget everything. He may have had a reputation for killing men, but he never did it without reason, and he never walked away and let it be for nothing.

So he was back where he started, even though he had successfully pushed them into making a move. Maybe it was time to talk to Stacy again, see if he could convince her that it was all over.

***

That same morning Stacy was waiting outside of Emma Cleary's boarding house for Mark Crawford. Instead, Emma came out and stood on the porch.

"What do you want, slut?" she demanded.

"I'm a slut and you're an old maid," Stacy said. "Now that we got that settled, why don't you go back inside?"

"Why don't you get away from my house before I come down off this porch?" Emma said.

Stacy was wearing one of her saloon dresses, although she was partially covered by a shawl she had around her shoulders. Emma Cleary had on a simple faded, blue cotton dress.

"Why don't you leave Mark alone, slut?" Emma asked.

"Why don't you find somebody your own age?" Stacy replied. "And besides, Mark's not as young as you think he is. He's no boy."

Emma started down the porch steps when the front door opened and Crawford came rushing out.

"Emma! Go inside."

"Are you goin' with her?" Emma demanded.

"I have to talk to her, that's all," Crawford said. Now go inside, and I'll be back later, after work."

"If I find out you've been with her—"

"To talk!" Crawford said. "I swear."

Emma glared at Stacy, who simply smiled up at her.

"This ain't over," Emma said.

Stacy waved her away. As Emma started down again, Crawford grabbed her arm and literally pushed her back into the house. Then he went down the steps and faced Stacy.

"Why do you have to get her worked up?" he demanded.

"Never mind her," Stacy said. "Walk with me. We have to talk."

"About what?"

"The Gunsmith."

"I thought you were takin' care of him."

"So did I," Stacy said, as they walked away from the house, "but last night he killed Merritt and Felton."

"Both of them? How?"

"They went after him in one of the girls' rooms, and he was waitin' for them."

"Is he in jail?"

"For what?" Stacy demanded. "Defendin' himself?"

"So what are we supposed to do now?" he asked. "The rest of the men aren't here yet."

"They'll be here," she said, "and then we're gonna put an end to this, and take care of that bank."

"What about the sheriff?"

"What about him? He's takin' his cut to look the other way.

At least, he thinks he is."

"Whataya mean?"

"You don't really think we're gonna split the take with Winslow, do you?"

"But he's supposed to pay the sheriff."

"Out of his cut," she said. "And if he doesn't get a cut . . ."

"But if the sheriff doesn't get paid, he'll come after us," Crawford said.

"You really think so?" she asked. "You've met Irving. He might go after Winslow, but he ain't about to get on a horse and come after us."

"So that leaves the Gunsmith," Crawford said, nervously.

"Mark," she said, "you just have to worry about doin' your part in the bank. When the rest of the men get here, we'll take care of Clint Adams."

"Wait, wait . . ." he said, grabbing her arm and pulling her into an alley, where he faced her. "If you're gonna doublecross Winslow and the sheriff, how do I know you're not gonna do the same to me?"

"Because I'm tellin' you who I'm gonna doublecross," she said. "Why would I do that if I was gonna doublecross you?"

"And the rest of the men?"

"They'll get their money," she said. "We're already saving some by not having to pay Merritt and Felton. The rest of the men weren't gonna get as much as they were."

Crawford studied Stacy's face, searching for the truth.

"Look, Mark," she said, putting her hand on his shoulder, "we came up with this idea, you and me. We're in this together. We always have been."

He put his hand on her and she did the unexpected. She pulled him close and kissed him.

"We're partners," she said.

"Partners?" he asked. "Is that all?"

She stroked his face.

"We'll see about somethin' else after we finish this job," she told him. "Just work with me, Mark. Trust me."

She gave him a big hug and when he leaned in for another kiss she backed away and put her forefinger over his mouth.

"Later, Mark," she said. "Let's save this for later. Meanwhile, you better keep Emma happy so she doesn't kick you out."

"Or make me pay for my room and board," Crawford said. "I got ya."

"Stay here a minute while I leave," she said. "And don't come to the River Run. If you wanna drink, go to the Black Horse."

"Yeah, okay."

She patted his arm. "This is all gonna work out, Mark."

"If you say so."

Chapter Forty-Two

Stacy had an idea.

Why not kill Clint Adams herself? She didn't care about reputations, she could just shoot him, leave him for someone to find, and nobody would be the wiser about who killed him. And they could get on with their business.

Because that's what it was for Stacy, a business. She had been robbing banks for a dozen years, using different men, and never anything hasty. There was always a plan and things always went off without a hitch, because she planned well. After her first two robberies, which had both ended with her running from a posse, she came up with this idea. Get herself established in town, scope out the bank, enlist the aid of someone local, use a few men, and get the job done.

And then Clint Adams had to show up.

If only she hadn't enlisted Mark Crawford a while back. He'd been running from posses for years, and when she approached him with her plan he had gone for it right away. Truxton, was their fourth job together, which was a little long for her, and Clint Adams appearing at the wrong time was proof.

It was time to get rid of Mark.

But first, the Gunsmith.

***

When Stacy reached the front of the River Run Saloon she found Clint Adams waiting for her. Her gun and thigh holster were in her room, so she said, "Lookin' for me?"

"I am," Clint said. "I knocked, but they said you were already up and out. I don't know many . . . saloon girls who get up this early."

"I had some errands to run."

She took out a key and unlocked the front door.

"You have a key?"

"All of us girls do," she said, "Harry wants us to be able to come and go."

"Harry?"

"The bartender."

"So the bartender owns this place?"

"No, Cade Dillon does, but he gave Harry a small piece. He doesn't wanna pay a bartender. What we do . . ." she shrugged. ". . . he can't do, himself."

She opened the door. "You wanna come up?"

"Sure."

She let him go in first, then stepped inside and locked the door. He followed her across the empty saloon floor, where chairs were piled up on top of tables.

"Harry should start takin' the chairs down soon," she told him. "Business as usual in a couple of hours."

She led him up the stairs, into the hall where he'd killed the two men, and to her room.

"Sit down on the bed," she said. "I have to get ready for my day."

He sat while she took off her shawl and sat in front of her dressing mirror.

"Takes a while to put my face on," she said, "and then comes the dress." She looked at him in the mirror, and then without touching any of the make-up on the table she turned to face him. "What do you need?"

"You sent those two men up here to kill me," he said.

"Go tell the sheriff."

"That wouldn't do any good," he said. "Not unless you admitted it."

"Which I'm not going to," she said.

"Right."

"So what do you want?"

"I want you and Mark Crawford to leave town, forget about your plan to rob the Bank of Truxton."

"What are you talkin' about?"

"Tell Winslow to find somebody else to help him rob his bank."

She stared at him, her face blank. He felt she was acting, but doing a damn good job of it.

"That's interestin'," she said. "You think the bank manager is gonna rob his own bank? No, that ain't interestin', it's rich! It's damn funny."

"Yeah, I thought so, too," Clint said, "especially when I figured out the sheriff is going to help him."

It became a little harder for her to maintain a stone face.

"What are you, some kinda fuckin' detective?" she finally asked.

"I've had my moments," Clint said, standing up. "It looks like I've got it all figured, Stacy, so my advice to you is to forget the whole thing."

He walked to the door, opened it, and turned back.

"If you don't, I'll stop you."

He went out. Walking up the hall he wondered what her next move was going to be?

***

Stacy was incensed.

She could have stepped behind the dressing screen to put on her dress for the day, and also hanging there was her gun and thigh holster. She could have shot him in her own room, and claimed he tried to rape her. Why hadn't she?

Not only did Clint Adams have it figured they were going to rob the bank, he had it all figured right!

How the hell had he done that?

And what the hell was she supposed to do now?

Chapter Forty-Three

Clint had the feeling he had truly put a burr under Stacy's saddle. If she had tried to have him killed last night, what would her next move be? How many more men could she send after him?

Now that he suspected Sheriff Irving of working with the Winslow to rob the bank, he had no one watching his back—not that he could have counted on Irving in the first place. So the thing to do now was fix it so nobody could have a clean shot at his back. And yet he wanted Stacy and Crawford, the sheriff and the bank manager all to know he was still in town.

He chose a tactic he had used several times in the past. He got himself a wooden chair, set it down in front of his hotel and sat with his back up against the wall, where he could see the entire street.

***

It took all her self-control for Stacy not to shatter the mirror in front of her after Clint Adams left her room. There was no way she could tell Mark Crawford the things Clint Adams had just told her. He would panic, for sure. And she couldn't go to Sheriff Irving, because he wasn't supposed to know that she knew of his involvement.

That left only one person she could go to.

She grabbed her shawl, wrapped it around her shoulders again, and left her room without touching her make-up. She took the hall to the back steps and went out the door.

***

The problem with sitting in front of his hotel was that, while everyone could see him, Clint couldn't see either saloon or the bank. There could have been a lot of activity after his visit to Stacy. She could go see the sheriff, or Winslow, the bank manager. No, probably not Irving. It didn't seem that anybody in town had confidence in their sheriff. The fact that he had been sheriff for many years was probably due to the town's laziness. They probably preferred the devil they knew.

That left Winslow. If Stacy was running the show, she must have gone to him early and convinced him to work with her. He probably even thought they were partners.

He decided to take up his position at the bar in the Black Horse Saloon, again. He hoped Leo the bartender wouldn't mind.

***

When Stacy opened the door to Winslow's office and entered, she could see he was surprised, and alarmed.

"You're not supposed to come here!" he hissed.

"Relax," she told him, "this is why you gave me the key to the back door, so I could come and go without anybody seein' me."

170

"Lock that door!" he snapped.

She turned the lock on his office door, then walked around behind him as he sat at his desk. She put her hands on his shoulders and rubbed. He sat back and sighed.

"What brings you here, Stacy?" he asked.

"Don't you think I might be here to see you?" she asked, running her hands down his chest, inside his jacket.

"I'm not a fool, you know," he said. "I know a beautiful girl like you wouldn't normally be interested in an old codger like me."

"Oh, come on," she said, leaning down and putting her mouth by his ear. "I knew when I first met you that you weren't an old codger."

Abruptly, she swiveled his chair around, fell onto her knees, undid his trousers, reached in and fished out his soft cock. She stroked and rubbed him until he was hard, then leaned forward and took him into her mouth.

"Ah, Jesus," he moaned, putting his hands on her head as she bobbed up and down on him.

It didn't take long, which was the way she preferred it. When she felt he was ready to erupt she released him from her mouth and caught his emission in the cloth she had brought along just for that purpose.

"There you go," she said, smiling up at him. "Not such an old codger, right?"

"All right," he said, hastily adjusting himself and buttoning up his pants, "what is it you need?"

"It's just a small thing," she said, standing up and moving around to the front of his desk. She discarded the shawl and leaned on the desk so he could look down the front of her dress—which he did.

"What small thing?" he asked.

"We need some men to take care of Clint Adams for us," she told him.

"Take care of him?"

"Kill him, darling," she said. "We need to kill him."

Chapter Forty-Four

When Clint reached the Black Horse it wasn't open yet. Neither was the bank. But there were some chairs nearby, so he snagged one and sat in front of the saloon, with his back to a wall, not a window.

Returning to his tried-and-true tactic, let them see you, and make them sweat.

He was sitting there about an hour and just as the bank unlocked their front doors, the door to the saloon opened and Leo, the owner and bartender, stuck his head out.

"You wanna come inside?" he asked. "We ain't open yet, but—"

"No, I'm good," Clint said. "Thanks."

"Well," Leo said, "how about a beer, or a cup of coffee? Least I can do if you're tryin' to keep the bank from bein' robbed. After all, I got money in there."

"I'll take a cup of coffee."

"Comin' up!"

Leo went back inside, reappeared moments later with a cup of coffee for Clint, and one of his own. He handed Clint his and then stood next to him, sipping.

"Think it's gonna happen soon?" he asked.

"If it happens," Clint said, "I hope it's soon."

"You gonna stop 'em all by yourself?"

"Looks like it."

"No help from the sheriff?"

"Apparently not."

Leo sipped his coffee audibly.

"I wish I could help, but I ain't worth shit with a gun," he said.

"That's okay, Leo," Clint said. "You do what you do, and I'll do what I do."

"I got an idea, though."

"Oh?" Clint looked up at him. "What is it?"

"Why don't you wait inside the bank?"

"I'll give that suggestion some thought," Clint said, handing the empty cup back.

"Another one?"

"Naw, I'm good," Clint said. "Thanks."

"See ya later."

Leo went back inside, closed the door for a short time, then opened the place for business. Every so often men would stop in, have a drink, and leave. The same went for the bank. But in all that time the only person he saw that he knew was Crawford, when he arrived for work. He didn't see Clint across the street as he entered the bank.

Inside the bank, huh?

***

It only took an hour for Nathan Winslow to send Stacy four men.

"I loaned them all money," he told her. "That is, the bank did. They'll do whatever you want for me to forgive the loan. Where do you want them to meet you?"

"Out behind the River Run," she said.

"Well, you go on over there," he said. "I'll have them to you within the hour."

So she waited, and they came, just as Winslow promised.

The four men rode their horses right up to her, and didn't dismount.

"You Stacy?" one of them asked.

"That's right."

"My name's Naylor, these are my boys." They were all the same age, so he didn't mean they were his sons, he meant they worked for him. "Winslow said you had a job for us."

"Kill the Gunsmith," she said. "That's the only job I've got for ya."

"Well, now," one of the others said, "that'd be a big reputation maker."

"And I can pay you," she said. "I'll give you a hundred dollars each."

"And our loans?" Naylor asked.

"Forgiven," she said, "that is, if you succeed in killing Adams."

"When?" Naylor asked.

"As soon as possible," she said. "Today."

"Where is he?"

"He's got a room over at the Truxton House Hotel. And he's been seen drinkin' in both the Black Horse Saloon and here at the River Run."

The four men exchanged glances, and Naylor turned to Stacy after the other three men nodded.

"You care how we do it?" he asked.

"No," she said. "Just get it done."

Naylor nodded, then he and his men turned their horses and rode back the same way they came.

"Naylor!" she called.

The man turned.

"Stay behind a minute."

Naylor told his men to go ahead and take care of their horses. He'd meet up with them, then turned his horse and rode back to Stacy, who had just been struck by an idea.

***

When all four men were gone Stacy went into the River Run Saloon through the back door, and up to her room. She hoped her problem would be gone by the end of the day.

Chapter Forty-Five

Clint realized there was no security inside the bank. Something like that had to be the manager's decision. He stood up and went inside the saloon.

"Ready for a beer?" Leo asked.

"Why not?"

The bartender drew one and set it in front of him. There were only two other men in the place, one at the bar, another at a table.

"Leo, you want to give me a hand?"

"With what?" the man asked. "It doesn't involve guns, does it? I'm more likely to shoot my foot off than do you any good."

"You don't have to touch a gun."

"Then I'm all yours," Leo said. "Is it about the bank?"

"It is," Clint said. "You probably know everything that goes on over there."

"Just because my business is across the street? And I can see it from my window very clearly?" Leo smiled. "You know I do."

"Can you tell me why there's no security in the bank?" Clint asked. "No bank guards?"

"There used to be."

"There did?"

"Sure, two of 'em," Leo said, "workin' in shifts. And they'd come in here for drinks before and after. If we were open."

"What happened to them?"

"I don't know," Leo said. "One day they just stopped coming."

"And you don't know why?"

"'fraid not," Leo said, "but you know who would?"

"Who?"

"The teller named Tilly," he said. "She's been working at the bank even longer than Nathan Winslow. She knows everythin' that goes on, and why."

"I've met Tilly," Clint said. "You're right, I should ask her."

"You can go back to sittin' outside. She'll be out at one, to go to lunch."

Clint raised his glass to the man and said, "There, you've been a big help, Leo."

"Anytime. Let me top that off for you and you can take it outside with you."

***

When Tilly came out Clint gave her time to put some distance between them and the bank, and only then did he approach her.

"Lunch?" he asked.

"I only have an hour," she said. "It will have to be just lunch."

178

"That's all I need," he said. "I have some questions for you."

She sighed. "I knew it wasn't for my womanly wiles. Come on . . ."

***

She took him to a restaurant he hadn't yet been to in town. At a back table they both ordered a sandwich and coffee, and then he got down to business.

"I'm curious," he said, "about why your bank doesn't have any guards inside."

"We used to," she said.

"That's what I heard," he said. "But why don't you, anymore?"

"Nathan let them go."

"When?"

"A few weeks ago."

"Did he say why?"

"I'm afraid nobody asked him."

"I see."

"Why do you think he let them go?"

"That's easy," he said. "To make it easier to rob the bank."

She looked concerned.

"You mean Nathan _is_ actually going to rob his own bank?" she asked.

"Or help do it," Clint said. "That seems to be the only reason he'd fire his security guards."

"So what are we supposed to do?"

"Well, I think it's going to happen in the new few days," Clint said. "If I was you I'd take some time off, Tilly. You don't want to be there when it all happens."

"Can't you stop it?"

"That's what I'm trying to do," he assured her. "You go home right after lunch."

"I should go back and tell someone—" she started.

"Don't tell anyone anything," he said. "Just go home."

"But there are female clerks working inside," she said. "And Mark—"

"Mark's part of it."

"That nice boy?"

He nodded.

"What about the clerks?"

"I'll try to keep them safe," he promised.

***

They ate their lunch, but neither had an appetite and they both left half their sandwiches. Tilly decided to take them home with her.

Outside on the boardwalk Clint said. "Now remember, don't go back to the bank. Go right home."

"O-okay." She started away, then turned back. "You'll come and tell me when it's all over."

"Of course," he said.

She nodded, turned and hurried home.

The Bank Job

Clint walked back to the Black Horse Saloon and once again took up his position in a chair.

It was there the four men—Naylor and his men—found him, and made their play.

Chapter Forty-Six

"That looks like him," one of Naylor's men said.

"Yeah, according to Stacy's description," Naylor agreed.

"How do we find out for sure?" another man asked.

"Easy," Naylor said. "I'll go and ask him. I want you three to spread out, make sure he can see you and you can see him. Leave this spot here for me." They were standing directly across from the seated man.

"What if he kills you?"

"Then you kill him," Naylor said. "Got it?"

All three men shrugged and one said, "Sure."

"Do we get your hundred dollars, then?" another asked.

"Take that up with Stacy," Naylor said, "or the banker. Now spread out."

***

Clint saw the four men directly across the street, watched as three of them spread out and the fourth started across the street toward him. From the look of the men it was easy to guess their game. They had been sent, either by Stacy, or the banker, or both.

Naylor stopped short of stepping up on the boardwalk. Rather, he looked up at Clint from street level.

"You Adams?"

"Who's asking."

"My name's Naylor," the man said, "Tom Naylor. You ever heard of me?"

"Nope."

"Well, I heard of you," Naylor said. "That is, if you're Clint Adams."

"I am."

"Well, whatayou know?"

"Is that a question?"

"You know," Naylor said, ignoring the question, "the man who kills you gets a big reputation."

"Many have tried."

"I ain't many."

Clint looked at the man's gun, riding low of his hip.

"You know how to use that?" Clint asked.

"I know how."

"Then you'll just have to be smart enough not to," Clint said.

"I always do the smart thing," Naylor said.

"Let's hope you're right."

Naylor stared at Clint for a few moments, then turned and started back across the street.

"Naylor!"

The man turned.

"They're not paying you nearly enough," Clint said. "Not nearly."

"Money ain't everythin', Adams," the man said, and continued back across the street.

Now all four men were spread apart, making it impossible to cover them at one time. Clint had encountered many men who felt stronger when they stood shoulder-to-shoulder. These men knew what they were doing.

But so did he.

Quickly, his eyes flicked about, looking for effective cover. Directly in front of him was a horse trough, filled to the brim. The water would absorb any bullets that punched into it.

Clint waited, watching Naylor. The other three were not going to move until he did.

Chapter Forty-Seven

Naylor drew his gun, and the others followed. As they fired, Clint threw himself out of the chair and behind the horse trough. A hail of lead slammed into the saloon wall where he had been sitting, also shattering some glass.

Then the target changed, and he felt the bullets slamming into the horse trough. They punctured the outside, getting slowed down by the water. As he lay there he could hear the water running out through the holes. If he stayed there until the horse trough emptied out, it wouldn't be the cover he needed, so he had to move.

"Come on out, Adams," Naylor shouted. "Let's do this in the street, like men."

"Like men?" Clint called back. "You mean like four men against one?"

Naylor laughed. "I like those odds."

"I don't!"

There was an alley alongside the saloon that seemed the most likely cover. Not yet with his gun in hand, he broke and ran for the alley. He heard shots behind him, as bullets whizzed by him but missed, once again slamming into the walls and windows of the saloon.

He stopped in the alley with his back pressed against the saloon wall. This time he palmed his Colt, fully intending to use it.

Nathan Winslow came rushing out of his office.

"What's going on?"

The two clerks and Mark Crawford were standing at the window, looking outside.

The teller turned and said, "Four men are shootin' it out with the Gunsmith."

"Is that so?"

Winslow walked to the window, stood next to Crawford and looked out.

"How interesting," he said.

"This is terrible!" one of the clerk's—an older woman— said. "Where's the sheriff?"

"Probably hiding under his desk," Winslow said.

When there were more shots outside, the two female clerks ducked down in fear. Winslow and Crawford exchanged a glance.

"Ladies," Winslow said. "I'm going to let you out the back. I want you to go home."

"In the middle of the day?" one of them asked.

"We don't know how long this will be going on out front," Winslow said. "I want you both to be safe."

"But Mr. Winslow—"

"Now, now, let's go." He herded them to the back and let them out the rear door, then returned to Crawford, who was still at the front window.

"Now's the time, Mark," he said.

"What? To rob the bank?"

"Yes."

"But Stacy—"

"Stacy's not here," the bank manager said, "and she probably sent those men to keep Adams busy. We have to act now! Come on."

Winslow hurried to his office, came out holding several large bags that were used to transport payrolls.

"I've kept these hidden for our use," he said. He handed one to Crawford. "Fill it from the teller's cages." He took his bags and headed for the vault.

Crawford didn't know what to do, but he was so used to being told that he went to the cages and began filing the bag with cash.

He carried his bag back to the vault, where Winslow was filling his.

"What do we do now?" he asked. "Where do we go?"

"Go? We don't go anywhere," Winslow said. "We're going to hide these bags in my office, and say that someone came in and robbed us while the excitement was happening out front."

"Do you think people will believe us?"

"Of course they will!" He took the bag from Crawford.

"But—"

"They'll believe us," he said, taking out a gun, "because you were killed during the robbery."

He pulled the trigger.

Chapter Forty-Eight

Clint knew if the four men were intent on killing him they'd have to follow him into the alley. When that happened, they wouldn't have room to spread out.

He turned, ran halfway down the alley and waited there behind a barrel.

***

"He's in the alley," Naylor said. "You three follow him."

"What are you gonna do?" one asked.

"I'm gonna go around to the other side," Naylor said. "He won't expect me to come that way. Now go!"

As his men followed Adams into the alley, Naylor looked for a way around the saloon.

***

Nathan Winslow checked the body of Mark Crawford to be sure he was dead, then hid the bags of cash in his office, and put his gun back in his desk drawer. That done he went to the front window to see how the action outside was progressing. He saw three gunmen run into the alley alongside the saloon.

Fools.

The Bank Job

As the three men entered the alley, they were virtually shoulder-to-shoulder. Clint stepped out from behind the barrel, gun in hand.

"That's far enough!" he snapped.

All three men stopped short and gaped at him. Their guns were in their hands but were pointing at the ground.

"Where's Naylor?" he asked.

None of the men replied, mainly because they didn't know who should. Naylor did all the talking.

"Come on, come on, one of you talk."

"H-he circled around."

"Makes sense," Clint said. "All right, how do you want to play it? Are you getting paid enough to die?"

The three men didn't like the sound of that.

"Come on," Clint said, "you've got your guns in your hands, I've got mine. Let's do it!"

The three of them stared at him, then without even sharing a glance they all threw their guns to the ground, turned and ran from the alley.

Clint turned quickly to look to the other end of the alley, but there was no sign of Naylor.

***

Naylor met Stacy behind the bank, where she had two horses.

"Is it done?" she asked.

"It's gettin' done," he said. "How do we get in?"

She showed him the key in her hand, then used it to unlock the door.

They went into the bank and crept toward the front. Stacy was wearing riding clothes, and had a holster around her hips. She had her hand on her gun, but removed it when she saw Mark Crawford on the floor. Then she saw Winslow at the front window.

"This wasn't the plan, Nathan," she said.

He turned and stared at her and Naylor with wide eyes.

"Neither was this," he said, gesturing toward Naylor.

"Well, Adams made it necessary to change the plan," she said. "Where's the money?"

"In my office," he said. "I was going to share it with you."

"I know you were. Let's get it."

Winslow hurried to his office, came rushing back out carrying three bags filled with cash.

"Take those," she told Naylor, then turned to Winslow. "Where are the ladies?"

"Tilly went to lunch, never came back. I sent the other two home, to keep them safe."

"How considerate. Did you have to kill Mark?"

"I didn't kill him," Winslow said. "The bank robbers did."

She stared at him a moment, then said, "Brilliant."

"I thought so," he said. "You know, we can really leave the money in my office and say that the robbers killed Mark and took it. Then we can split it, later."

"That sounds like a nice plan," she said. "Except for one thing."

"What's that?"

She drew her gun.

"The bank robbers killed you, too."

***

Stacy had Naylor put Winslow's body in front of the vault, to make it look like the robbers had killed him there.

"Okay," she said, "now we can get out of here."

"What about my men?"

"You wanna split this money—and me—with them?" she asked.

"No," he said, giving her a hungry look.

"Then let's go."

As he headed for the back door with the three bags of cash she shot him in the back.

***

When Stacy came out, lugging the bags of cash, Clint said, "I had a feeling you adjusted your plan."

She stopped short and stared at him.

"Well," she said, "you pretty much ruined the one I had in place."

"Where's Mark?"

"Dead."

"And Winslow?"

"Dead."

"And Naylor? Don't tell me . . ."

"Dead."

"You're really something, lady."

"Me? Come on, don't tell me Naylor's men ain't dead."

"They're not," he said, "but they're miles from here by now, and probably still running."

"Well then," she said, "what now?"

"Are you wearing a gun?" He couldn't see her hips with the money bags held in front of her.

"Yes."

"You want to drop those bags and go for it?"

"Hell, no," she said. "I want you to put these bags on the horses, and then you and me can ride. You can have the money, and me."

"You know, that would be tempting," he said, walking to her, plucking her gun from her holster and tucking it into his belt then backing away, "if I didn't have to wait for you to try and shoot me, at some point. You see, Stacy, your reputation definitely precedes you."

"So what now?"

"We walk to the sheriff's office."

That made her happy. "Okay, fine."

"Oh, I know you think Irving will be with you," Clint said, "but not after he hears about Mark and Winslow and Naylor. No, he'll toss you in a cell and be the hero who stopped the bank robbery. At least, that might get him a raise."

That thought made her decidedly unhappy.

Chapter Forty-Nine

"Wait," Sheriff Irving said. "You're tellin' me you think I was involved with the robbery?"

"What I'm telling you is, here's the money," Clint said, putting his hand on the bags he'd dropped onto the sheriff's desk, "and now you've got Stacy in a cell. And you have a bank full of dead people. The rest is up to you, Sheriff."

Sheriff Irving looked at the three bags of money.

Clint leaned forward and placed his hand on the man's shoulder.

"I know you'll do the right thing and get yourself reelected."

Clint turned and left, then stopped.

"Oh, and one more thing," he said. "If it was you who took that shot at me the other night, I forgive you."

Outside, he headed for Tilly's house to give her the news that she was probably going to be promoted to bank manager.

***

"I heard all that!" Stacy called from inside her cell. "Come on in here, Sheriff."

Irving tore his eyes away from the money and walked into the cell block. He was not wearing his gun.

Inside the cell Stacy pressed herself up against the bars and smiled at him.

"You can have the money," she said, "and me. Whataya say?"

She could see he was riding the fence, for the moment.

"Come 'ere, Sheriff." She reached out, grabbed his belt and pulled him forward, then pressed her hand to his crotch. "Lemme help you decide."

She undid his trousers.

Coming Soon!

THE GUNSMITH
433
Little Amsterdam

For more information
visit: www.speakingvolumes.us

On Sale Now!

THE GUNSMITH
431
The Science of Death

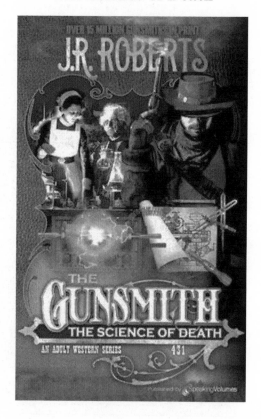

Visit us at <u>www.speakingvolumes.us</u>

On Sale Now!

THE GUNSMITH
430
Show Girl

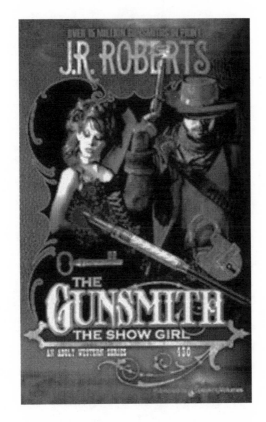

Visit us at

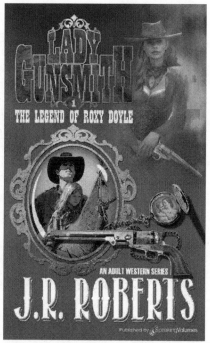

Coming Spring 2018

Lady Gunsmith 5
The Portrait of Gavin Doyle

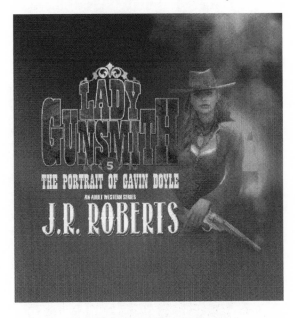

For more information
visit: www.speakingvolumes.us

On Sale Now!

ANGEL EYES *series*
by
Award-Winning Author
Robert J. Randisi (J.R. Roberts)

Visit us at <u>www.speakingvolumes.us</u>

On Sale Now!

TRACKER *series*
by
Award-Winning Author
Robert J. Randisi (J.R. Roberts)

On Sale Now!

MOUNTAIN JACK PIKE *series*
by
Award-Winning Author
Robert J. Randisi (J.R. Roberts)

Visit us at www.speakingvolumes.us

Sign up for free and bargain books

Join the Speaking Volumes mailing list

Text
ILOVEBOOKS
to 22828 to get started.

Message and data rates may apply.

90754100R00125